Enfrascada

by Tanya Saracho

FOR PRODUCTION ENQUIRIES

UNITED STATES AND CANADA
Info@SamuelFrench.com
1-866-598-8449

UNITED KINGDOM AND EUROPE
Plays@SamuelFrench.co.uk
020-7255-4302

Each title is subject to availability from Samuel French, depending upon country of performance. Please be aware that *ENFRASCADA* may not be licensed by Samuel French in your territory. Professional and amateur producers should contact the nearest Samuel French office or licensing partner to verify availability.

MUSIC USE NOTE

Licensees are solely responsible for obtaining formal written permission from copyright owners to use copyrighted music in the performance of this play and are strongly cautioned to do so. If no such permission is obtained by the licensee, then the licensee must use only original music that the licensee owns and controls. Licensees are solely responsible and liable for all music clearances and shall indemnify the copyright owners of the play(s) and their licensing agent, Samuel French, against any costs, expenses, losses and liabilities arising from the use of music by licensees. Please contact the appropriate music licensing authority in your territory for the rights to any incidental music.

IMPORTANT BILLING AND CREDIT REQUIREMENTS

If you have obtained performance rights to this title, please refer to your licensing agreement for important billing and credit requirements.

ENFRASCADA was first produced by Teatro Luna (under the title *Jarred*) from November 6 through December 14, 2008. The production was directed by Tanya Saracho, with set design by Tim Thomas Jr. and costume design by Christine Pascual. The Production Stage Manager was Ana Espinosa. The cast was as follows:

YESENIA/ROMINA.................................. Yadira Correa

CAROLINA ....Tanya Saracho

ALICIA..Dana Cruz

LULU/WOMAN............................Marie Antoinette Flores

CAT/MARTA/KARINA .... Miranda Gonzalez

CHARACTERS

YESENIA

CAROLINA

ALICIA

LULU

CAT

ROMINA

MARTA

WOMAN

KARINA

Note: Characters can be doubled. This is especially recommended for the "Señora Track" (**CAT/MARTA/KARINA**).

SETTING

Chicago, IL and the surrounding area

TIME

It could be now, but mainly this is set in 2013. But it could be now.

AUTHOR'S NOTE

Overlapping is very important in this play because these women – these friends – they talk over each other, finish each other's sentences, and can listen as they talk; you know, as Latina girlfriends do. Overlapping is denoted by a /. A // indicates a cue to the same speaker.

Scene 1

WISCONSIN OR BUST

*(Wisconsin. An outdoor concert. You can hear a band kind of setting up and sound checking. **YESENIA** is setting up a blanket on the grass. **CAROLINA** is looking toward the musicians, every so often stomping her left foot.)*

YESENIA. I don't know why we didn't stop at the damn Citgo. / Seriously.

CAROLINA. Because you're always on Potorro time.

YESENIA. I hate doing things when I'm thirsty. I think I died de sed in a past life.

CAROLINA. She went to get you water. / You're a fish.

YESENIA. …Little ass bottles. What are they gunna sell here? Just those little bottles. Cost an arm and a leg too.

CAROLINA. *(Still looking toward the music stage.)* Stingiest rich person I know. Hey, is that one yours? That one with the dreads?

YESENIA. Dreads? No! Wait, which?

*(**CAROLINA** points.)*

No way! Ugh. Can't stand white people with dreads. Why do they do that to their head?

CAROLINA. Only the dirty ones do it. Cochinos.

(Beat.)

Yessie, I think we're overdressed. I'm looking around and I'm thinking we're a little too decked out.

YESENIA. We're in Wisconsin, we could be in PJs and we'd be too decked out. Fuck, these shoes are no good for

7

this grass. Why didn't I wear my kicks? I'm gunna take 'em off.

CAROLINA. Gúacala de pollo, luego se te meten bichos entre los dedos.

YESENIA. There's gonna be bichos, Carolina. We're outside. Is that what you're doing with your foot there? Killing bichos?

CAROLINA. Shut up, you know what I'm doing with my foot.

YESENIA. Still?

CAROLINA. Am I pregnant right now? No. Do you see a belly on me? No. So I'm going to keep on stomping my foot, thank you very much. I don't want to talk about it.

> *(Beat.)*

Oooh, is he that one with the pelito like this? All Justin Bieber?

YESENIA. His hair don't look like Justin Bieber. Does it?

CAROLINA. All over his face like this?

> *(Makes gesture. They crack up a little.)*

YESENIA. Man, shut up. I'ma throw this shoe at you.

> (**ALICIA** *enters carrying four waters. She tries to hand one to* **CAROLINA.**)

ALICIA. Something just dawned on me. As kids – here you go Caro – as kids or in our formative years, we are never taught Grace. That woman who just shoved me to get to the head of the line; no Grace. / And what is that? It's like our parents, our grandparents teach us obedience and something akin to a code of ethics but do they ever truly teach us – *(Handing two bottles to* **YESENIA** *as she continues.)* Sorry, they only had this size – // do they teach us Grace? Is that a notion that is… Sorry. That's all they had. That's why I brought you two.

YESENIA. Some cheesehead shoved you?

YESENIA.
(*To* **CAROLINA.**) See? What did I say? Little ass bottles.

CAROLINA.
(*To* **ALICIA.**) That's not going to be enough for her. She's a fish.

YESENIA. How much were they?

ALICIA. Girl.

YESENIA. They were like five dollars each, weren't they? Just like at the movies. / This water better taste like Cristal!

CAROLINA. Coda.

ALICIA. Listen. I just had the idea of the year! Well for me it is because I've been wracking my brain trying to think of a theme to pitch on Thursday –

YESENIA. I just hate it when people are shady. / Descára'os.

ALICIA. It's a concert, Yesenia. The prices are going to be shady. Come on don't start gettin' the stankface, girl.

CAROLINA. She does get her stankface.

    (*Beat.*)

What theme? Like for a party?

ALICIA. No, like we do every year at the museum. The thematic. What's the season going to be about. Like next season, it's Fear, which is just so totally sexy. I mean, the kind of programming we're about to bring in surrounding the theme of Fear is just –

CAROLINA. What's this year's?

ALICIA. Oh, this year is lame. You were at the opening night party, remember? It's another look at the 60s in Chicago. / It's nothing. We do it every few years in one configuration or another. People just like to see blown up black and white photographs of '68 and the Democratic Convention and Mayor Daley and riots. Complete sensationalism if you ask me. Anyway, like I said, 2012 is Fear, which is like…just so exciting to me.

CAROLINA. Oh, right! We wore the beehives to the party! That was fun.

YESENIA. Fear's exciting?

ALICIA. Just as a theme. But what I'm trying to say is that I think I got 2013!

YESENIA. My credit card expires 2013 and it always feels so far away.

CAROLINA. You can like make that happen? Decide what the whole MCA has to do for the year?

ALICIA. Kind of. I mean, after last year I sort of can. In this new position, yeah. But I still have to pitch it and they have to like it.

CAROLINA. What's 2013 going to be?

ALICIA. Grace.

CAROLINA. What like…when you pray at the table?

ALICIA. That's when you *say* grace, but sure. Maybe an exhibit will have something to do with saying grace. Sure. I hadn't even thought of it.

YESENIA. Like ballerinas. They're very graceful. But they got busted ass toes because they have to dance around on their tippies. *Black Swan*, girl.

ALICIA. Yeah, that idea of Grace too. I mean… What does Grace look like? What are the elements, the markers of…is it a value, an instinct. I don't know. I'm just talking here. This is so great. I'm so glad we came out here, Yess. You see what clean air does? We need to get out of the city more often. Breathe in all this air. This pure oxygen is good for the brain.

> (To **YESENIA**, who's sitting holding the two bottles like the Holy Grail.)

What's the matter with you? I thought you were thirsty.

CAROLINA. There's that stankface again.

YESENIA. Feels like I need to ration these bottles or something. Man, my past life, I know I died in the desert.

CAROLINA. There's more water right over there, ridícula.

ALICIA. Yess, I'll go get you more water. Come on. Look at all this. How can you have a stankface with all of this? Look at this sky! So blue and so clear. We got this nice spot in the shade. We got our blanket. We got our... little waters. I got these cheese curds. / Apparently they're all the rage here. I got you chips. And here we got us. All set up and ready to listen to your new man play in his –

CAROLINA. Is that what that is?

YESENIA. He's NOT my man.

ALICIA. Right. Not your new man, but your new...what? Um...

CAROLINA. Lover.

YESENIA. See?! / I knew you guys were going to be like this. I knew you guys were going to make a bigger deal about this than it is. He's not my anything...

ALICIA. Alright, alright not your man, not your lover. Your boy toy? / No, not boy toy... Um, your FRIEND. We're here to see your *friend* play in his band.

CAROLINA. Bootycall-on-call?

Her friend is the one that looks like Justin Bieber over there.

ALICIA. Oooh, is that him?

(*Pause.*)

YESENIA. Yes. He's the one that looks like a short lesbian.

ALICIA. He's not that short.

YESENIA. Short to me. You know I like 'em of NBA dimensions. Can we stop staring at him, please? You guys are gettin' me all... Just come on. Could you just sit down? He's going to see us and I didn't say for sure-for sure that I was coming. You too Caro. Sit chu ass down. Stomp later. When they start playing you get up and stomp, okay? You making me nervous.

(*They settle.*)

ALICIA. I love summer.

CAROLINA. Our one month of it.

ALICIA. But isn't it so worth it? People don't take it for granted here.

YESENIA. I always think that. People other places take the sun for granted. When I go back to Puerto Rico I always think, "You don't know how good you got it here."

ALICIA. I should do something like this with Diego. We haven't gone out in so long. I mean, not even to like a restaurant. He's been so depressed and I haven't pushed because I've been so damn busy.

CAROLINA. It's hard when the woman's the breadwinner, isn't it? Real talk. If it's hard when the man is the breadwinner like in my case, I can only imagine how it is for you.

ALICIA. He'll find something again.

YESENIA. Of course he will. That's my boy. He just having a bad year but I got a couple of little candles lit for him. You'll see he'll bounce right back.

ALICIA. Candles…we need some of these companies to call him back for an interview, that's what we need. Not candles.

CAROLINA. Sometimes candles can get a company to call him back, Alicia.

(Quick beat.)

Let me stop. You never like talking about all that stuff.

ALICIA. Just worried about him. It's hard to celebrate all the good stuff that's happening to you when your guy won't get out of his sweats because he's so down.

(Beat.)

Yessie, these shoes are sickening.

YESENIA. Aren't they tho'? Half off, girl.

CAROLINA. How do you always find the deals!

*(**CAROLINA** is still trying to stomp her foot while she's sitting down.)*

YESENIA. Can you please…

    (CAROLINA stops.)

ALICIA. I should call Diego. I want him to TiVo that show about honey bees.

    (She tries to call.)

    Are you guys getting reception?

YESENIA. AT&T, girl. Una mierda.

ALICIA. It won't even let me send a text. This is crazy.

CAROLINA. Can you imagine a world without texting?

YESENIA. Yeah, apparently it's called Wisconsin. Here, let me turn it on and off. Sometimes that works.

    *(**ALICIA** hands her iPhone to **YESENIA**.)*

ALICIA. Oooh, good idea.

CAROLINA. This Brazilian straightening is really holding up in this weather. I'm like amazed. I can't stop touching it.

ALICIA. I know. You look like a Pantene commercial. I'm getting one. Looks so good on you.

CAROLINA. Right? You need to go to this girl. She really knows what she's doing. You too Yesenia. Te lo alacia if you want.

ALICIA. No! I like her hair natural. Don't do anything to it, Yessie.

YESENIA. I'm done doing shit like that to my hair. Can't ever do shit with this pelo malo. All my sisters have good hair like you guys but me, I'm born with the pelo malo. / I gave up. I just concentrate on the shoes.

ALICIA. I love your hair.

CAROLINA. I never understand why you call it that, Yessie.

YESENIA. I'm not going to go through five hundred years of colonization with you again, Caro. You don't listen. Here, Ali. I think you got bars now.

ALICIA. Oooh, thanks. I'm just going to call Diego real quick. Tell him we're staying the night, right? We're staying the night?

(They nod. **YESENIA** *is carefully drinking and examining her water.* **ALICIA** *dials. The band starts to play.)*

CAROLINA. I think they're starting. What kind of music does he play?

YESENIA. I don't know.

CAROLINA. He didn't tell you?

YESENIA. I never asked. Talking is not our thing.

ALICIA. Hello? I'm sorry I have the wrong...

(She checks the screen to see if she dialed right.)

I'm sorry...

(Beat.)

Excuse me? Who is this? Can I ask why you are answering my house phone? Can you put Diego on the – Excuse me? Who are you?

(The band is playing full force, but **CAROLINA** *and* **YESENIA** *are staring at* **ALICIA,** *focused on whatever the hell this other person on the line is saying.* **ALICIA** *is trying to catch everything. Her face has fallen and is Casper white.)*

Can you please put Diego on the phone? What do you mean he's... Put Diego on the –

(Beat.)

Diego...baby, what's going on? Why is there a woman answering our landline?

(Pause.)

You what?

(The band hits some loud sections. The three are frozen in "oh, shitness." Lights out.)

Scene 1.2

REFLECTIONS OF A LULU #1

*(Two areas. In one, **LULU** is bouncing on an exercise ball. She's got a couple of books by her feet and is eating something healthy from a Gladware container. She's in a bathrobe, wearing sunglasses indoors. She wears a leather belt with her bathrobe. In the second area, **ALICIA** is standing frozen, eating Häagen-Dazs straight from the container. She continues eating throughout **LULU**'s interstitial.)*

LULU. Love is the engine. There is proof. The things that remain from past civilizations? Expressions of Love: A temple, a tomb, a painting. Love is poetry and novels and rap songs and web pop-ups. Love is science. The same part of the brain that rules Love is the one that controls addiction. By that definition, Love becomes an addictive substance. So a breakup is the purest form of withdrawal and should be treated with the same care as an addict going *cold turkey*. With the same respect.

(Bouncing pause.)

Cold turkey. Note to self, look up the etymology of the term "cold turkey."

(She jots it down without getting off her ball. More bouncing. Lights down.)

Scene 2

CALL TO ACTION

(A few days after the Wisconsin concert. Back in Chicago, Pilsen to be exact. Doorbell. LULU runs to let YESENIA and CAROLINA in, who are carrying tons of ALICIA's stuff.)

YESENIA. …Did he put rocks in here? Even pulling this shit with the wheels is heavy as hell.

CAROLINA. Because we're going up, so wheels are not going to help. I told you I would pull that one.

(To LULU.)

Sorry. Hi. You're the cousin! Hi.

LULU. I'm the cousin.

CAROLINA. I'm Carolina. This is Yesenia.

LULU. Carolina. And Yesenia. I'm the cousin.

YESENIA. Does the cousin have a name?

LULU. Oh. Yeah. She does. I do. I'm Lulu. Comein comein.

CAROLINA. Thank you for…

(To YESENIA, who's still at the threshold.)

Yessie, just come in already. Qué dramática.

(Back to LULU.)

Sorry. Thank you for putting Alicia up. We've heard so much about you. / I always wanted to go to UofC, it seems so Ivy League…

YESENIA. We have? I still don't know why she's not staying with me. No offense to you, but I have three bedrooms and this isn't exactly The Drake right here.

CAROLINA. Yessie!

YESENIA. You. You have Vic. I get it. I get why she wouldn't want to stay with you, but me? I got three fucking bedrooms. / You need space when you're dealing with shit.

CAROLINA. Family is family, Yesenia. I'm sorry, we're all... You know, we're all kind of like a little crazy right now with the whole – Poor Ali. Feel so bad for her.

LULU. Aristophanes said that "One must not try to trick misfortune, but resign oneself to it with good grace." Things will work themselves out, I think.

YESENIA. But does she have to come work them out en la punta del demonio?!

CAROLINA. Ya Yessie! Enough with all that sass today. She's a little grouchy pants right now. Sorry. Is Ali here?

LULU. Therapy.

CAROLINA. Oh, really? She's doing that again. Okay.

YESENIA. Sangano descarado, que se pudra. Pero si se me cruza ese hijo de su / puta madre...

CAROLINA. Yessie, what did we say in the car? It's not going to work if you're like this in front of Ali. You're taking it worse than she is. Aplácate.

YESENIA. I swear to God I almost threw up in his face. Couldn't stand to look at him. For how many years now...for how many years –

CAROLINA. I know...

YESENIA. Every Monday night – every Monday night I'm at this fool's house watching the game. / Every Monday night. This is my guy, you know? That's my guy. Fucking asshole.

CAROLINA. I know...I know. I know.

(*Beat.*)

YESENIA. I can't fucking handle this shit...

CAROLINA. Imagine how la pobre de Alicia must feel.

YESENIA. I can't. If I feel like I've been stabbed through the throat, I can only imagine.

CAROLINA. Lulu, how is she doing? I meant to check in with her yesterday but –

(LULU's about to answer.)

CAROLINA. Oooh, Yessie. I remembered what I was trying to say in the car. Vic gave in. About the house. Yesterday he woke up and was like, "Baby, let's buy that place you've been wanting." I was like, "Ohmygawd!" I didn't even mind his morning halitosis and rewarded him the way only I know how. Sorry, Lulu. Graphic.

(To **YESENIA***.)*

Can you believe it? We're going to look in Wicker Park. And if Vic's saying get a three-bedroom, you know what that means, right?

(She stomps her left foot a few times.)

I need to keep at this. Even if all the other stuff is freaking me out, I'm going to keep at this.

YESENIA. Start the registry at Babies "R" Us, my friend.

CAROLINA.   YouWillSayYEStomeYouWillSayYEStome YouWillSayYEStome…

(She stops. Tired herself out.)

This one definitely took longer than the ring, man. He's a hard one, my Victor.

(To **LULU***.)*

Sorry, we're talking code. Not being rude.

YESENIA. *(To* **LULU***.)* Where's your belt? I mean the one that goes with your bata.

LULU. With my what?

YESENIA. With your robe.

CAROLINA. Yessie, que mal educada.

LULU. Oh, I guess I lost it.

YESENIA. You look like a skinny Santa Claus or something.

LULU. Oh, yeah? I guess I do.

YESENIA. What are you wearing under there?

CAROLINA. Yessie! You're just meeting the girl!

YESENIA. What the hell's she wearing under there?

CAROLINA. Eso es muy su asunto. Can you sit down, please? You're making me nervous.

(*To* LULU.)

Sorry, we're not usually this...aggressive. Hey Yessie, did you think... I don't know. I didn't think that tacky little skank / would look like that.

YESENIA. Descarada. I swear to God I wanted to punch her on her fucking nose.

CAROLINA. Her?! Punch him!

YESENIA. Gringa descarada.

CAROLINA. But did you think she'd look like that? I don't know why but I thought she'd be prettier. She's got a nose like Miss Piggy.

YESENIA. Busted ass white girl. She looks like she don't shower.

CAROLINA. Why would he leave Alicia for that? There's no comparison.

YESENIA. She's white that's all. No offense Lulu.

LULU. None taken. I'm only half.

YESENIA. Hope you were raised by your good half.

CAROLINA. I will say though, Yessie. She does have a good body. Tacky little skank.

YESENIA. Please.

CAROLINA. (*To* LULU.) She's got those gringita legs like they have, you know? All shapely. / Like a Rockette.

YESENIA. Descarada / sitting there in shorts.

CAROLINA. Girl, was it me or did she look sixteen?

YESENIA. Hope that fucker gets crabs. Those kind of girls always have crabs.

(*To* LULU.)

Fuck, when's Ali supposed to get here? I have a showing at six.

LULU. Her session should be over.

CAROLINA. (*To* LULU.) Lulu, how does she seem to you?

LULU. *"Grief walks upon the heels of pleasure."*

(*Beat.*)

CAROLINA. …

LULU. She's fine, I think. Or rather, she'll be fine. Cookie?

(*She offers them the box of cookies.* CAROLINA *takes one.* YESENIA *refuses.*)

CAROLINA. Thank you.

YESENIA. What do you mean fine? Without the Sudoku, please.

LULU. I don't know. She seems fine to me. A little down maybe, but that's to be expected. Been sleeping in a lot. I come home from class and at least the past couple of days, she's just been kind of conked out.

YESENIA. She hasn't gone to work?

LULU. Not that I know of.

YESENIA. What about the whole Grace thing? She has to do the Grace thing…

CAROLINA. Ella no es así.

YESENIA. I know. She's like a geek about work. Fuck.

LULU. But not to worry. It's been nothing very dramatic. No big bawling sessions. And if she hasn't cut her own bangs, she's all good. We've just been eating a lot of falafels because I just learned to make them out of chickpeas. Oh, and soup.

(*She eats cookies.*)

YESENIA. It hasn't hit her. That shit's going to hit her like a ton of bricks. Y todo porque se le metió a Diego esta pinche gringa –

CAROLINA. You know, I'm not usually the type to hate on white girls. That's like so 1992, you know? My friends in high school were all a bunch of Beckies. I mean, in Texas, what else were they going to be, you know? And two of them even stood up at my wedding and everything. I'm not a hater. I *like* white people.

YESENIA. That's cuz you didn't grow up in Chicago.

CAROLINA. And Beckies are usually fine by me. No offense Lulu. You're only half a Becky.

LULU. I'm half a Becky. A Hecky. *(Little weirdo.)*

CAROLINA. *(To* **LULU** *about the suitcases.)* Lulu, where do you want these?

LULU. Just anywhere for now. When she gets back we can ask her what's up.

CAROLINA. *(To* **LULU.***)* So, Ali tells us that you're getting your PhD, huh? / That's great.

YESENIA. Aaaarrgg, smug ass bitch has the audacity to speak to me! I almost scratched out her eyes. I'm not doing too good with this. Fuck. Do you have any Tums?

*(***CAROLINA** *looks for one in her purse.)*

LULU. Tums taste yummy to me. I wonder if you could make a dessert out of Tums.

CAROLINA. I just can't believe Diego. Just letting her sit there with Bandido on her lap? Como todo una reina on her throne.

LULU. The dog switched camps too, huh? That's going to be tough.

YESENIA. That bitch already thinks she owns the place.

CAROLINA. Which makes me think: How long has this been going on, you know?

LULU. The mystery thickens. Cookie?

*(***CAROLINA** *takes another cookie.* **ALICIA** *enters.)*

YESENIA. Hey, girl. I got a workout too coming up those stairs.

(Just a weak smile from **ALICIA.** *Kiss salutations all around.)*

CAROLINA. Hey, Chiquis.

(Pause.)

How was the shrink?

(**ALICIA** *shrugs. An awkward pause.*)

LULU. "*There is no better than adversity…every heartbreak, every loss, contains its own lesson.*"

    (*Beat.*)

Malcolm X.

    (*Weird beat.*)

YESENIA. You got yourself some lunch?

LULU. We still have the bisque. I learned to make corn bisque.

ALICIA. No thanks, I ate a little something.

CAROLINA. We got all your stuff.

ALICIA. Not *all* my stuff.

CAROLINA. Well, we got what he packed for you.

ALICIA. Thanks guys. Thanks for doing that for me.

CAROLINA. Oh, please. Not at all.

ALICIA. Well, I appreciate it.

YESENIA. Girl.

ALICIA. Was he…

CAROLINA. He was there. He gave me some mail for you.

    (*Taking out some mail from her purse.*)

ALICIA. Thank you.

    (*Beat.*)

Was she?

YESENIA. Yeah, girl.

    (*Beat.*)

ALICIA. Hhmm…

    (*Long beat.*)

Were they…

    (*Beat.*)

Was she –

LULU. She was wearing shorts and was sitting on the throne with your dog Bandido. Did I say that right? She has nice Rockette legs but a pig nose.

YESENIA. Oye, ¡tú!

LULU. That's what she's asking. I'm just reading the writing.

ALICIA. Yes, cousin. That's what I was asking.

> *(Beat.)*

Sitting with Bandido, huh?

CAROLINA. Yeah. On her lap.

> *(Long beat.)*

YESENIA. And why does Diego get to stay in the apartment, huh? / You should have made his ass leave! His triflin' ass… Let's see if this little putita will put him up with her McDonald's money or whatever the fuck she does.

CAROLINA. Yessie. Yessie. Yesenia! What did we say in the car? What did we say!

> *(Pause.)*

ALICIA. He's got no job. I'm not going to put him out, Yesenia. Please. Just…please.

CAROLINA. Did you have a good session?

ALICIA. I guess. I've gone three times this week and she just sits there not saying anything.

YESENIA. Well, might take a little longer than three days. Therapy's not magic.

LULU. Therapy's good. I've had a shrink since I was twelve. It's good.

ALICIA. I can see what she's doing and it's not helping. Talking is not what I need right now. I do need something, but talking is not it.

CAROLINA. Maybe you need a new person.

LULU. You're not liking yoga?

CAROLINA. Yoga?

ALICIA. Lulu's got me going to yoga with her in the mornings, right Lulu? It's not bad actually. It's okay. I

don't know… I just. I'm a little bit… I don't want to
bother you with my – / I mean, you already have gone
above and beyond here. I can't believe I sent you to get
my things. I just don't want to cause any uncomfortable
moments since this girl apparently…

YESENIA. Girl.

>   *(Beat.)*

Girl.

>   *(Beat.)*

Girl, please.

ALICIA. Apparently lives in my house now. If I didn't have
you get my clothes, maybe she'd be wearing them too.

YESENIA. We need to find out this girl's name.

CAROLINA. For Facebook stalking? I agree.

YESENIA. No. You know what for.

CAROLINA. Oooh.

YESENIA. You and me. We're going to take care of this.

CAROLINA. Okay.

YESENIA. We go to your Señora.

CAROLINA. Nononono, we go to your Señora. My Señora
right now is on some other… She's on this dark path /
and I rather…

LULU. What's a Señora?

ALICIA. Guys, seriously. None of that. I'm sorry, but I need
a real fix. I don't need like fantasy things that don't
actually –

CAROLINA. They're not fantasy things at all, Ali.

ALICIA. Listen. I came home from Wisconsin to find her
in my bed. In my bed, Caro. He knew I was coming
back and he didn't get her out of there. He knew. They
both knew and it's like he staged it. Like one of those
model homes, he staged it. Had the fireplace going. It's
not even cold. Had candles and bottles of wine and a
blanket on the… God! Why can't I cry.

>   *(Beat.)*

I'm standing there with the mail, because why did I get the mail? What made me think, "Oh, we need to look at our Chase bill"? Acting like… I don't know. But I stand there and all Diego can say to me is, "I'm sorry, Alicia. I didn't plan for this to happen." And that was it.

CAROLINA. Oh, he's got the candles / and he didn't plan for this to happen?!

YESENIA. What is this, *Days of Our* fucking *Lives*? "Didn't plan for this to happen."

ALICIA. How did this happen?

CAROLINA. Girl. It's nothing you did.

ALICIA. No, I mean, HOW did this happen?! I want to know the logistics. I'M OBSESSED WITH THE LOGISTICS RIGHT NOW.

CAROLINA. I'm telling you. We go online. / Every thing is online. Her address, misdemeanors…

ALICIA. No. I mean, in my house. I want to know every detail, every moment. I want to read the schedule of events, like in a file or something. I need a play by play of the chronology. When did they meet? How? When did she first come into our apartment? What made it okay to bring her there? Fuck. I can't think of anything else. Yesterday at work, it took all of me yesterday to…let's just say it's pretty hard to pitch the concept of Grace when all I can think of is, does he pet her hair in front of the TV while they watch the Discovery Channel? Aaarrgg.

> (*Beat.*)

Nine years of my life and he won't even sit down and talk to me. You guys know that's not Diego. That's not him.

YESENIA. Está embruja'o.

ALICIA. (*Beat.*) How the heck do people do this? How do people get over something like this?

LULU. "*The only cure for grief is action.*"

> (*Beat.*)

G.H. Lewes

> *(Weird beat.* **LULU** *puts a big handful of cookies in her mouth.)*

YESENIA. I'm going to tell you what action we're going to take right now. Okay? I'm going to send you to my Señora. I don't want to hear it. You going to yoga with this one, going to that therapy that's not going to help any. Sorry, but that white people shit is not going to help any. You're going to my Señora.

CAROLINA. Shut up Vic and I go to therapy.

ALICIA. The woman who can tell you your future? No, that shit is not for me, Yessie.

YESENIA. Yeah. That one.

ALICIA. I don't believe in all that. No offense to you, Yess, but I just don't believe in that.

YESENIA. Okay. Not that one, then. But just indulge me. Hazlo por mí, nena. I'll take you to one that's real good. Es una morenita, but she's real good with things. You'll see.

ALICIA. Yess, I'm sorry.

YESENIA. Ali? This bitch was in your bed.

> *(Beat.)*

Bandido.

> *(Beat.)*

On her lap.

> *(Long pause.)*

ALICIA. Oh, God. This is so stupid…

CAROLINA. She'll go.

YESENIA. That's my girl.

> *(Taking out a bottle from her purse.)*

But in the meantime, a little Jose Cuervo to get us through the day…and my closing.

CAROLINA. Yesenia, there's a lot we need to teach you about tequila. This stuff is crap.

YESENIA. I know you a tequila snob / but we all going to drink it right now. I got some cups right here in my purse.

(The next two lines overlap.)

ALICIA. I don't feel like drinking right now...

CAROLINA. Preparada y toda la cosa.

YESENIA. Yup. Always prepared.

(YESENIA hands ALICIA a cup.)

ALICIA. Oh, God, Yess...

YESENIA. Come on. You too over there, in your little batita. Come on.

(LULU comes over and takes the last of the four cups. They raise their cups.)

To the wise women.

(They all say a loud "Salud." They react to the tequila going down.)

LULU. *"Better than the pain of thinking, Is to steep the sense in drinking."*

YESENIA. Okay, don't give this one any more.

Scene 3

THE TWO-HEADED CAT

(A humble kitchen in the South Shore of Chicago.
CAT *is leading* **ALICIA** *to the kitchen table. There's
some sort of construction paper project with maps
on the table. It's very involved.)*

CAT. Just through here, Honey. Go on ahead and sit down
– How did you find me again?

ALICIA. Yesenia Rivera, she was the one who… She
recommended you. She was actually supposed to come
with me but she –

CAT. Hold on, Honey. Romina, come and get this shit up
off of this table.

(*To* **ALICIA**.)

I'm sorry about that, my daughter always keeps this
house a sty with all her shit everywhere.

(*Offstage to* **ROMINA**.)

Romina, what did I tell you about putting your mess all
over my table? Romina!

ROMINA. Chill out. I was coming out to get it as soon as I
heard the doorbell. / I know how you get.

CAT. Don't you sass me. Got the nerve to get your back up
about it.

ROMINA. Chill out.

CAT. You better fix that face or I'll fix it for you. Alright
now. Excuse my daughter, she got a attitude.

(*To* **ALICIA**.)

Go ahead Honey, sit right there. We'll get you going as
soon as this girl gets her shit up off my table. Slow as
molasses.

ROMINA. I was doing a project. I got a system going.

CAT. I ain't got all day here.

(ROMINA finishes and exits.)

CAT. I'm sorry about that. That's my pride and joy right there, but you have to have a firm hand with kids now days. Ooh, can I get you some water? Some juice? We got some cherry soda.

ALICIA. Aaah...

CAT. Romina! Will you get this girl some juice from the porch?

ROMINA. *(Offstage.)* What kind?!

CAT. What kind you want, Honey? We got grape and apple. You want a pop instead?

ALICIA. Water's fine, thank you.

CAT. Just bring in some iced water for the both of us!

(Beat.)

See, you're lucky I ain't one of them bad doctors. You shouldn't ever take anything that don't come off a can or a closed bottle from any rootworker. That's rule number one.

(ALICIA is suddenly panicked.)

Oh, don't worry, Honey. I'm not one of them swindlers. To show you, I'll drink whichever glass of water you want me to. We don't lay down those tricks in this house.

(ROMINA enters with the waters.)

Thank you, Hon. Make sure you finish your work now.

ROMINA. What you think I'm trying to do?

CAT. Is that sass?

ROMINA. No, ma'am.

CAT. Go on ahead then.

(She exits. ALICIA's looking at the water.)

Pick one, Honey, I'll take either one.

ALICIA. Oh, it's okay. This one's fine.

(She takes a drink.)

CAT. So-he-broke-your-heart, huh.

ALICIA. I'm sorry?

CAT. Some fool broke your heart and here you come looking for me to get him back.

ALICIA. Actually, I'm just here to have a kind of anthropological experience.

CAT. You said who?

ALICIA. I'm just here for fun. Hhmm...curiosity.

CAT. Some fool didn't break your heart?

ALICIA. It's a little more complicated than that –

CAT. It is never as complicated as all that. Either you want to *get* someone, or get someone *back*. That's all there is, really. You might also want to get back *at* someone. But I don't think that's why you're here. No. Vengeful eyes didn't come through my door today. You come in here looking like a wet noodle about some fool who broke your heart and you want to get him back. Is that about right?

ALICIA. Like I said. It's a little more complicated than that.

CAT. You got kids?

ALICIA. No. No, ma'am.

CAT. Then it's not as complicated as all that.

> *(Beat.)*

> Let me tell you one thing, sugar. Before we get started and I tell you what I CAN do, it's good we talk about what we SHOULD do. Look, I don't know your situation. But if you got no kids and he up and left and was rotten to you / I suggest you do all the bawling you have to do. Then you go ahead and get good and mad. Throw things, eat ice cream. Get yourself piss drunk, buy some – I don't know – get yourself some shoes like they wear on *Sex and the City*. Get you some good dick. Nothing better to cure the blues than some good dick. Do all the things you got to do.

ALICIA. He wasn't rotten to me...

> *(Beat.)*

CAT. Then let it go. That's not magic, that's just common sense.

    (Pause.)

But that's not why you're here, is it? Nope. Okay. One day you'll remember my words and you'll realize that the best thing you can do is to just let him go.

    (Pause.)

But not today. Alright then. Let's have it. He yo husband?

ALICIA. No. My partner of nine years. We've lived together for seven of those years and we had just become engaged. We hadn't set a date yet, but –

CAT. He like yo husband you live together seven years –

    *(Loud song is heard from **ROMINA**'s room.)*

Romina! Turn that racket down! Put on your damn earphones.

ROMINA. It ain't even loud!

CAT. Romina I swear for God!

    *(**ROMINA** turns music off.)*

Thank you! Lord.

    *(To **ALICIA**.)*

Alright, so you want this fool back. Well, girl, first you have to have him WANTING to come back. Got to make him restless for you.

ALICIA. How do I do that?

CAT. Did he leave you for another woman?

    (Pause.)

ALICIA. Yes.

CAT. Anthropological…

ALICIA. …

CAT. What she got? Money? Big titties? Does she turn him out? Does she go down on him with ice cubes or Alka-Seltzer or something?

ALICIA. What...

CAT. Guys are into all sorts of stuff nowdays. I bet she give him the ass. They always trying to take that ass.

ALICIA. How would I know?

CAT. My ex-husband always trying to take that ass.

ALICIA. She's young. Like twenty-four. She's living with him now. In our apartment.

CAT. Ah, hell no! Alright, let's see. Alright. We're gonna do the "Intranquil Spirit" spell on him. We're going to Intranquil him until he can't help it but come back.

ALICIA. I'm sorry, is that bad? I'm actually not sure if I want to do any of this. It was my friend's idea that I come see you. I think I'm wasting your time... I'm sorry.

(ALICIA *has gathered her things and stood up.*)

CAT. Sit down. Sit down.

(*Beat.*)

You a broken li'l thang, aren't you?

ALICIA. I'm not saying I believe in any of this but if I did, I wouldn't want to get bad karma.

CAT. You don't believe, huh? Yet here you are. You must believe something.

ALICIA. Is what you're suggesting like black magic? I don't want to do black magic.

CAT. There is no black or white magic. And there is no karma in hoodoo. We don't believe in all that mess.

ALICIA. I don't want him hurt. This is the man I love, you know what I mean? He's not like a random bad guy or something.

CAT. Well, look at you. I swear I never saw nobody come in here and they man leave for another woman and they not asking, "Can you make him lose his job?" "Can you make his dick fall off?" Usually if they man cheat, they come in here wanting to do all sorts of things on him.

ALICIA. You can do that? You can make someone's penis fall off?

CAT. Girl, if you knew what people come in here asking. And yes, a cucumber and some nails will lay that trick. Why you not angry at him? Girl, you should be piss mad.

ALICIA. I don't know. When I caught them together. I wasn't angry. I was just confused. This is Diego. This is the guy I've picked. We've just made all these plans to spend our lives together and... I'm sounding like a Lifetime movie right now. Sorry. I just...I just want to make it like it was. As long as it's not something evil, I want to make it like it was.

CAT. And "like it was" was so good, huh?

ALICIA. Yes.

> *(Beat.)*

...yes.

CAT. Hhmm... Tell you what. I'm going to do the "Intranquil Spirit" for you and I'll throw in a "Bitch Be Gone" for that little tramp. Make that bitch be good and gone forever. That still won't fix you two when he does come back, but we'll worry about that when we come to it. For that I will charge you $125 and I like you, so I'm going to give you a spell to do on your own that will probably help more than most anything. This spell is older than almost any spell I know. This spell, it's in the Bible, girl. You ever made a honey jar?

ALICIA. No, of course not. I've never done any of this.

CAT. Write this down. Here some paper. Here go a pen. You take a jar. Any jar. You put a whole thing of honey in there, two cinnamon sticks, and some brown sugar. Then you tear off a piece of brown paper bag write his name on it, then you put your name in a circle trapping him nine times –

ALICIA. Whole name?

CAT. Yeah, his whole God-given name. Written clockwise. You close it up real tight. So tight. Then every day. Now you gotta do this EVERY DAY. You shake it. You shake that honey jar. You shake it and you think lovely things.

You think about when he used to make love to you, when he used to rub your feet and tell you nice things. You think about the times he made your leg shake like a doggy. Anything that you can feel in your body. Put all you energy into this honey jar, to sweeten him back to you.

(*Dead serious, very clear.*)

And no matter what. No matter what, you NEVER ever open the jar. Listen very carefully, you open the jar, the whole thing sours. You understand that?

ALICIA. Yes, ma'am.

CAT. While you do that, I'll be working on your "Intranquil" and your "Bitch Be Gone." And no, that's not a necessarily nice spell. But you leave that one to me.

(*Loud music again.*)

ROMINA! IF I HAVE TO TELL YOU ONE MORE TIME ABOUT THAT MUSIC –

(**ROMINA** *enters.*)

ROMINA. It ain't me. I don't even like Lil' Wayne. It's them again.

CAT. Getting on my last good nerve. I think it's time we hotfooted those two.

ROMINA. I told you. Should've hotfooted them a long time ago.

CAT. I was trying to be Christ-like and turn the other cheek...

ROMINA. Just give me the powder, I'll take it upstairs and lay the trick right now.

CAT. Can't hear myself think. Romina, go on an' bang on the ceiling will you?

ROMINA. (*Exiting.*) Oh, I'll go bang on they heads if you want. Don't be letting people study in this house.

CAT. Sorry 'bout that. What was I talking about? Oh, the "Bitch Be Gone." Ah, that noise. Honey, don't you worry none about that. I'm going to toss that tacky little

bitch in the river and drive her skanky ass away from
your life. Like I'm 'bout to do to these people upstairs.

ALICIA. In the river?! No. No, I don't want her to like be
hurt or anything –

CAT. Honey, I'm not actually tossing HER in the river. I
make a dollbaby – a poppet with some mean herbs in
there and I toss that in the river. Maker her go away.

ALICIA. Oh, my God. Like a Voodoo doll?

CAT. Yes, like a Voodoo doll only I'm not Vodoun. It's fine.
It's not like they show in the movies. Don't think she
going to start breaking off at the limbs or something.
You want your man back, don't you?!

ALICIA. I'm just...I'm nervous! I don't...I've never done
something like this before!

(The music is turned off.)

CAT. Thank you, Lord!

(To ALICIA.)

Please, everybody always says they never done something
like this and they been doing things since the day they
were born.

ALICIA. This is like a spell you're about to do. / I've never
done a spell in my life.

CAT. Do you cross your fingers for luck?

ALICIA. Yeah.

CAT. Do you knock on wood?

ALICIA. Yes.

CAT. That's a spell. Do you wish on a star?

ALICIA. Aaah, I used to.

CAT. That's a spell. Do you find a penny on the ground
and save it for good luck? When you sneeze, do you say
"God bless you"? Have you ever caught the bouquet at
a wedding so you'll be next down the aisle?

(Notices ALICIA's reaction.)

Sorry, we'll skip that one. You see what I'm saying
though?

(Beat.)

CAT. Nothing but spells. You're doing them, you just don't realize you're doing them. Don't you be worried.

(Music starts up again.)

I swear to God…I swear they just got on my last good nerve.

ROMINA. Mama, I can't study like this.

CAT. I know, Honey. I'm about to take out the Goofer Dust.

ROMINA. Take it out Mama. You've given them warnings enough.

CAT. I do like the grandma so much, it ain't her fault her granddaughter's a mess.

ROMINA. Oh, well Mama. So mote it be! SO MOTE IT BE!

CAT. *(To* ALICIA.*)* Honey, we're going to have to cut this visit a little short. We 'bout to hotfoot us some hoodrats.

(Lights down.)

Scene 3.2

REFLECTIONS OF A LULU #2

(Two areas. In one, LULU is sitting on the exercise ball. She's got a couple of books by her feet and is eating Whole Foods cookies. She is bouncing less this time, rolling more. In the other area, ALICIA is carefully putting things into a jar, reading off the piece of paper with the recipe. By the end of LULU's interstitial, ALICIA gives the jar a shake. Not bad.)

LULU. If you think about it, we've been the same humans since the beginning of time. I don't think we've truly experienced much in the way of evolution…if you really think about it. Well, advances in technology, sure. Fire; the wheel; the iPhone. Sure. But in basic terms, we haven't leaped significantly as emotional beings. Still territorial; still threatened by foreigners; still irrational. We are the same primitives. That's a little depressing, that we are basically the same humans.

(She takes a bite of her cookie.)

Same concerns: Shelter. Reproduction. Sustenance.

(Bite.)

Fiber. All still necessary to us as organisms.

(Looking in ALICIA's direction.)

Only now we put it in little cookies and sell it to one another for exorbitant amounts.

(Lights down.)

Scene 4

SECRET(ito)S

*(Two weeks later. We at the club. We at Ñ to be
exact. The unpretentious Latinorati hangout on
Elston Ave. Cute Brazilian girl DJ playing all the
cuts.* **CAROLINA** *and* **YESENIA** *are decked out to
the nines. The shoes are everything.)*

YESENIA. Look at that situation going on over there.

CAROLINA. Pathetic.

YESENIA. I know.

> *(Drinks.)*

We can remedy.

CAROLINA. Vinimos a lo de Ali, Yesenia. We're here for
that.

YESENIA. But while she gets back, we can be here for THAT.

> *(She drinks from the little straw, hard. Then she
> starts to dance to the music in the direction of the
> dude.)*

CAROLINA. Oh, here we go. I'm going to feel sorry for this
dude by the end of the night, aren't I?

> *(***YESENIA*** really brings out some good moves. It's
> kind of hypnotizing. Not funny hypnotizing, this
> shit is deep.* **CAROLINA** *lets it go on for a bit but
> then tries and struggles a little to get* **YESENIA** *back
> to the highboy table.)*

Yessie, the girlfriend is giving you the stank eye. Ay,
don't be chusma. Ven acá that I don't want to end up
in a fight with anybody's woman tonight. Come on. I'd
like to be able to come back to Ñ, thank you very much.
Ven te digo.

YESENIA. Ay, what! You cock blocker. Bueno, to be
continued.

CAROLINA. I want to tell you something. And I don't know if I should wait for Ali to come back from the bar cuz it's the kind of thing…YESENIA. Over here please? I'm saying something serious. I don't know if to wait for both of you guys to be here at the same time or to like…I don't know, tell you and you tell me if it's a good idea or not to even tell her.

YESENIA. Okay, what did they put in your drink? Didn't understand a fucking word / you just…

CAROLINA. This is seltzer water.

YESENIA. Shit. Well, then that's the problem! Let's get you a real drink! You like those fruity martinis, you want one of those?

CAROLINA. No, I can't drink. For at least nine months I can't drink. That's what I'm trying to tell you!

> (CAROLINA *indicates stomping her left foot a few times.*)

YESENIA. Oh, shit…

> (ALICIA *enters, two drinks in hand. One for* YESENIA, *one for her.*)

CAROLINA. Pero tú cierra el pico, okay? Wait till I tell her.

ALICIA. The bartender was acting like he didn't know me. I hate that.

CAROLINA. He's bitchy. I think he's on the DL. His eyebrows are too plucked.

ALICIA. They are a little too plucked.

CAROLINA. He probably goes to get them threaded. Cabroncito.

YESENIA. Look at that situation over there. She's dancing like a fool and he's just sitting on that stool bored. What a waste.

CAROLINA. I think she's a passer. A real Latina wouldn't be moving her hips like that.

ALICIA. *(Loaded.)* Moving like *how*?

CAROLINA. Exactly!

(CAROLINA mimics the rhythmless girl a little bit; a moment of levity.)

YESENIA. *(To ALICIA.)* Look at you, out and about. That's good, girl. / Can't get you out of the house lately.

CAROLINA. I know! And with the cutest top! Where did you get that?

ALICIA. Akira. It's old.

CAROLINA. So cute.

YESENIA. Oh, man she didn't just do the cabbage patch! Where is she from?!

(They react to the rhythmless girl. A moment.)

CAROLINA. Everything okay? I've been trying to call you all week.

ALICIA. I know. I'm sorry. I've been meaning to call you back. I'm in the middle of all that 2013 planning. So now I got Fear and Grace fucking up my life at the same time. I've just been having to be two steps ahead of everything, you know?

CAROLINA. Yeah, but like…after work? I mean, you don't text back? ¿Qué onda?

YESENIA. You been too busy eating soup with Lulu? /

(Back to the bumpkin.)

Look at this bitch…

ALICIA. Shut up Yessie.

YESENIA. Just saying.

CAROLINA. What are you up to? It feels weird not to see you all the time.

ALICIA. I haven't been up to anything, just…you know. Just doing things. This and that.

YESENIA. This and that?

CAROLINA. Like what? I'm not being metiche. I swear.

ALICIA. Just things.

YESENIA. Oh, you mean like "things"?

CAROLINA. Oh, I get it.

ALICIA. What? No.

>   *(Beat.)*

Is it DJ Nova tonight?

YESENIA. Ah, the avoid.

CAROLINA. She's ashamed. You're ashamed.

ALICIA. Y'all, please.

CAROLINA. Ali, are you thinking this is country? This is not country.

ALICIA. Not country, but there's something...I don't know...underdeveloped / nation –

YESENIA. Like retarded?

ALICIA. No, you know just from a less civilized time.

CAROLINA. You're saying it's country.

YESENIA. Jibaro, shit. It ain't just Jibaro shit.

CAROLINA. But it works, and you're freaked out aren't you?

ALICIA. I don't know if it works. Everything could be coincidence. I don't know.

YESENIA. Claro que it works. Generations swear by it! They're going to be wrong? I don't think so.

ALICIA. Generations swore the Earth was flat too, Yess.

>   *(YESENIA puts out her hand so ALICIA can talk to it. She continues dancing a little bit.)*

CAROLINA. Alicia, remember when my sister Elena couldn't get pregnant?

ALICIA. ...

CAROLINA. When Elena couldn't get pregnant for ever and ever, and she was devastated? Remember? Our Señora made her pregnant. Elena had been trying to get pregnant for five years and nothing. Every procedure. Every drug. All these painful things being stuck up her coochie... But this Señora, in her little tiny Little Village apartment, in her kitchen floor, she did these things... Shook her belly; la sobo; she did like this to her.

>   *(Demonstrates.)*

CAROLINA. Then she tied a red ribbon around her waist with this coconut looking thing and said, "Five weeks you'll be pregnant." Five weeks. She was pregnant.

ALICIA. Yeah, but who's to say it wasn't some lucky sperm that finally made it through?

CAROLINA. It wasn't lucky sperm! She had stopped doing all that fertility stuff. No. This is real. Every time there's something serious the doctor won't or can't cure. My whole family, we go to her.

YESENIA. Sometimes I rather go to my Señora if I got something crazy going on with my body instead of some quack doctor. What do they know? They just invented medicine not too long ago, these ladies have been doing it for hundreds of years. That I trust, Ali. Wise women. Oooh, I like this song!

CAROLINA. So nothing this hoodoo woman is doing is working?

ALICIA. I didn't say that…but I don't know what "working" means.

　　　　　(Beat.)

I can't believe I'm on this side of the conversation right now, but yeah I guess in a way, something's working. You guys, it's so weird. I see myself doing these things that this woman tells me to do.

CAROLINA. How is she? I've never been to her.

YESENIA. She's good! What you think I'm going to recommend her to a buster? Isn't she good, Ali?

ALICIA. I think so but I mean, what do I have her to compare to, you know? I've actually only seen her a few times.

CAROLINA. Wait, so it is working if you're seeing her a few times…

ALICIA. It's just…interesting to me, some of the things she says, I mean. And some of the things she has me do. It's so funny, I see myself going to buy these things, herbs and I don't know, brown sugar and catnip and random things like that and I do these, well, I'm going to call them meditations. She keeps saying "conjurings" but I think of them more like meditations and just that act, the act of meditating into this jar…I don't know. There's something that centers me about that. All this anxiety and shit I've been feeling just kind of pours into this jar and turns into the opposite thing. I spend hours shaking this jar and looking into it, figuring out how we got from point A; to point B; to here. Because I'm like a fucking sleuth, piecing it all back in my head, trying to put the pieces together. So I'm there, shakingthatjar, shakingthatjar.

    (Beat.)

But then something happens and I snap out of it and I think, "I'm shaking a fucking jar." I'm sitting here, at my cousin's place – bless her soul, she's great – but it's not my own place that I bought and decorated with my partner of… I'm just sitting here, staring into a fucking jar waiting and hoping this shit works.

YESENIA. Well, you don't have to just wait and hope. You can get you a little divination check up. Un little update status. Who sings this?

ALICIA. A what?

CAROLINA. She's saying you can get your cards read.

YESENIA. Her Señora's the one to go for cards. I mean, her Señora is a beast! She's never been wrong with me. Only now she won't take nobody.

CAROLINA. Yeah, not my Señora right now…

YESENIA. Why all of a sudden not your Señora?

CAROLINA. How about your Doña Martha, the woman with the water?

YESENIA. Madrina. Yes! We'll take you to my Madrina! There's no better kitchen Santera in all of Chicago. I'm telling you.

ALICIA. The water?

YESENIA. Yeah, she reads the water. It's intense.

ALICIA. Like from the faucet?

YESENIA. Nah, girl. In a fishbowl. But there's no fish involved. Doña Martha was the one who told this one about Vic. Remember, Caro? Right after we graduated, Doña Martha saw him in the water and described him to a T.

ALICIA. Shut up.

CAROLINA. No, de veras. She called it. Down to the big Aztec nose.

ALICIA. She actually saw him in the water?

    *(**CAROLINA** nods.)*

YESENIA. But to reel him in wasn't so easy, was it? For that she needed the big esoteric guns and so she went to her curandera. Now she got him right here, mira.

    (Points to the palm of her hand.)

CAROLINA. Shut up, Yessie. You make it sound so manipulative. He just needed a little shove getting to where he was going to get to anyway. Shut up. I shouldn't have told you anything.

ALICIA. Yeah, no thanks. that sounds a little too intense for me, I think. I might just stick with my little honey jar. I just want to…I don't know, to fucking figure out how we got here.

YESENIA. *(About rhythmless girl.)* What is she trying to pole dance with that chair? That girl might need an intervention.

CAROLINA. What exactly do you have that hoodoo woman doing for you? Is she doing you a trabajito?

ALICIA. How do you mean a "trabajito?"

YESENIA. A spell.

CAROLINA. I don't like the term spell.

ALICIA. Um, yeah. She's doing something. She's doing prayers over one of those tall candles and she gave me this sack thing that I'm supposed to carry to make Diego get all distraught and tortured so that he has to get in contact with me. We just started all that this week, so now I can't answer any of his calls or texts. That's part of the whole spell thing. He has to contact me three times but I can only answer after the third time. If not it won't work.

CAROLINA. Oooh, you did the "Intranquil Spirit"! Every aunt of mine has done that one. It's very good for wandering husbands that travel a lot. It works.

    (To YESENIA.*)*

She does have to wait, Yessie.

YESENIA. Oooh, okay, then you got to wait. I wonder if in the meantime you could have her put a curse on that white girl. You need her name and birthday though.

ALICIA. Oh, I got her name.

CAROLINA. Shut up, you do? Did you make a fake profile and friend her?

ALICIA. Um, no. Diego told me. Well, he said it the time he let me walk Bandido.

YESENIA. He LET you walk Bandido? LET YOU? That's your dog! / He ain't shit...

CAROLINA. Oh, see he's talking to you now! That's good, right?

ALICIA. Sort of. We talk about the logistics. Mostly we text. But that one time with Bandido he did bring up her name.

YESENIA. Sangano desgracia'o.

ALICIA. Her name is Bethany.

YESENIA & CAROLINA. *(Loud reaction.)* BETHANY!

CAROLINA. Bethany?! Oooh, that's her name? I hate her so much more right now. Could she be more gross?! I knew a girl named Bethany in high school and her breath always smelled like pickles and she had camel toe. Didn't she have a mirror? Bethany is a bad news name.

YESENIA. Girl, now we know her name. We can handle our business. We can fuck this Bethany bitch up!

ALICIA. God! No Yessie!

YESENIA. Not like, fuck with her credit or jump her in an alley. I mean, we can fuck that bitch up metaphysically.

ALICIA. Absolutely not. Even thinking that is crazy, okay?

YESENIA. Okay. For now.

CAROLINA. It sounds crazier than it is, girl.

(A moment while they're engaged with the sights and sounds of the lounge.)

ALICIA. So you said that your Señora predicted Vic, huh? I mean, like she described him or did his face actually like appear in the water?

YESENIA. No girl. She saw him in there. In her own way.

ALICIA. Does that mean that she has more powers than the hoodoo Señora?

YESENIA. It's not like powers. What is this *Charmed?* They're called gifts.

ALICIA. Well, maybe I should still see her and see what she says.

YESENIA. …

ALICIA. What do you think your Señora would say, Yessie? Will you take me to see her?

CAROLINA. Sometimes it's not good to see more than one Señora for the same problem.

ALICIA. But maybe she can look in the water for me.

YESENIA. You shouldn't mix and match just yet, since you're doing multiple things with the rootworker.

ALICIA. No, come on. I'm just curious about the whole water thing. Will you take me?

YESENIA. Hhhmm, I'll think about it.

ALICIA. Yesenia.

YESENIA. *(Dancing.)* …

CAROLINA. Maybe it doesn't hurt to take her.

YESENIA. Fine. I'll take you, but right now will you let me shift this percolator elsewhere? How much you want to bet I can go home with dude?

ALICIA. I would lose that bet, Yess.

CAROLINA. I think dudette will have a little something to say about that.

YESENIA. Yeah, like maybe she'll want to come along too. Two-for-one. Oh, BAM!

    *(**YESENIA** resumes her snake charming salsa moves.)*

CAROLINA. Oh, Lord Ali. Take off your earrings and your rings. This isn't going to end well.

    *(**ALICIA** is amused, **CAROLINA** worried. But also, this happens every time. A quick moment where **CAROLINA** holds her belly. Lights down.)*

Scene 4.2

REFLECTIONS ON A LULU #3

(**LULU** *is sitting at her couch/chair again. Books all about her.*)

[*Coming to a theater near you.*]

Scene 5

CHACHA

(**MARTA** *is reading the water as the lights come up. A* **WOMAN** *is sitting with her hand over the fishbowl filled with water.*)

MARTA. …I told you before he's a mariquita. You don't want to listen; you don't want to listen. Pero en el agua te sale que él es mariquita.

WOMAN. But he loves women. And that's actually the problem Doña Marta, him loving women so much.

MARTA. Ha, he love women! He love women and he love men. Es gubarron. El es gaycito con los cabroncito'. No sea' ciega. Qué tú quiere que yo te diga, ¿chacha?

WOMAN. (*A bit too loud.*) Men are not the problem Doña Marta, it's all these women that keep –

MARTA. Sssh, que the neighbors. Ssshh. You know they want any reason to go complain, siempre con el oido para'o. Okey, I just telling you. Ponte las pilas porque un patito te lo quita –

(*Knock on the door.*)

Ssshhh.

(*Knock again after a pause.*)

¿Quién?

(*To* **WOMAN**.)

If they don't speak no Spanish I don't open. ¿QUIÉN?

YESENIA. Soy yo Yesenia, Madrina.

MARTA. Aaah, Yesenia. ¿Por qué tu tocas así, chacha? You going to give me the high blood pressure.

YESENIA. Discúlpe usted. ¿Está ocupada?

MARTA. No, pasa pasa. Pasen rapidito –

(*Closes door.*)

MARTA. Qué luego the neighbor – you know how that one is. No pintan nada but they in everybody's bizne'.

(Referring to the one across the hall.)

You know yesterday she had there two men, un tipo in the morning y el otro in the night. Two men. Sin vergüenza. I bet she didn't even shower between them. Y la prieta de arriba que no se calla. Middle of the night she come from work and making her noise with the hippity hop. I call the landlord but you know everyone afraid of the blacks now so they don't do nothing. Nobody want to kick the blacks out because they sue you o empiezan a molestar. But I take care of it my own way. I take care of it. Tomen asiento, sit sit. Just a little bit. We almost finish.

(Back to water reading.)

Bueno chacha. Where were we?

WOMAN. Que Hector was gay, you were saying…

MARTA. Asi, más pato que los que vuelan, mi niña. And of that you won't cure him.

(Something else comes up in the water.)

Tú tiene' problema' con las kidney?

WOMAN. No, I don't think so.

MARTA. Chekate las kidney. Porque veo algo. Algo por aquí por las kidney.

(Beat.)

Okay, any questions?

WOMAN. Aaah, mmm. No, I think that's it.

MARTA. Bueno, cójelo con take it easy and chekate las kidney, ¿okey mi vida? Y pa'lante. Póngase las pilas.

WOMAN. Thank you Doña Marta. I'll see you…maybe next month.

MARTA. That's good, that's good. Y cuidado con ese patito.

WOMAN. Alright…bye bye.

*(To **YESENIA** and **ALICIA**.)*

Bye.

YESENIA. ...Bye.

MARTA. *(Closing door.)* She need to leave that gaycito de su husband. I didn't want to tell her but he might be sick with that disease de los gays. She don't believe me though. Every time I tell her y la gente don't believe when I tell them.

> *(Beat.)*

¿Y tu grandmother? How is my comai doing with her diabetes?

YESENIA. She's doing okay Doña Marta. They put her on dialysis last week.

MARTA. Ay, bendito. Tell her I'll light a candle to San Lazaro for her health. Todos vamos directito para allá, que se le va a hacer. You can't escape old age. ¿Se van a leer las cartikas?

YESENIA. Not me Doña Marta. This is my friend Alicia, she really wanted to come consultar the water con usted. She doesn't speak much Spanish.

ALICIA. Hello.

> *(Pause.)*

I understand it though, well, a lot of it. I understand a lot of it.

MARTA. *(Puts her hands on her head and face.)* Hhmmm... hhhhmmm. Okey. So sad, esta niña que me traes. But she can't cry. She stuck. The tears are stuck inside her head. You been crying?

ALICIA. Actually, no.

MARTA. You will. And it will be a good thing. Acuérdate de mí. Vas a llorar un océano, nena. Those tears is exactly what you need to let out all this thing you got carrying inside. In fact, that might be the only thing you need and is wrong with you. Nesecita un good cry.

> *(Beat.)*

MARTA. Bueno, let's take a closer look. A ver, póngame la manita. On top of de guater.

>   (**ALICIA** *puts her hand on top of the water.*)

I see you floating. You don't have no home right now. Yea, I see you floating.

>   (*Beat.*)

Ah, you had a husband, no, not a husband. Tú andabas con un trigueño lava'o.

ALICIA. What's that?

YESENIA. Like a light brown dude.

ALICIA. Yeah...yes. He is kind of light brown.

MARTA. Sí, con un sangano bueno pa'na. Okay, I see what happened. Este tipo a trobomeike.

ALICIA. I'm sorry?

YESENIA. A troublemaker.

ALICIA. Oh, no. He's good. He's a good guy. He doesn't make trouble...not like with the law or anything.

MARTA. You can't lie to me. I know he wasn't always so good to you.

ALICIA. No, he's not a bad...he's a good guy.

MARTA. Pero sí aquí está en el agua, chica. Not the first time he did this with another girl before. He did it lots of times to you before. You can't lie to me.

>   (*Pause.*)

¿Miento?

>   (*Pause.*)

YESENIA. Is that true?

ALICIA. Yeah...

YESENIA. Ali.

MARTA. So why you love him so much si este es un sangano desgraciado that didn't deserve you?

YESENIA. Diego cheated on you before? Why didn't you ever tell us?

MARTA. Sshhhtt. Uste' cierre el pico que este reading's for her not for you.

(Beat.)

MARTA. ¿Tú sabe' qué pasa? You think there is no other man in the ocean. Pero mi'ja as soon as you get you some new cuchichi with somebody else, se te olvida este cabrón descara'o.

ALICIA. I don't want another…cuchi chuchi. I want him back. I actually don't think there is another man in the –

MARTA. Ay, chacha. ¿¡Pero por qué?! Estás comiendo de lo que pica el pollo.

ALICIA. Is there something you can do for me or not?

YESENIA. Girl.

MARTA. Who do you think you talking to? Of course there is sumsing I can do. You mean business, eh.

(Beat.)

Bueno, pero primero nos vamos a get rid of this putita con quien se junto.

(Phone rings.)

Me cago en el coño de la gata.

(She picks up.)

¡Alo! ¿Quién eh'?

(Beat.)

Ah, no speak English. Sorry, no speak no English. Adiós. Goodbye.

(Beat.)

If they speak me in English les cuelgo. Bill collector. Or they try to sell me something. Yo estoy en un bodge. I am a woman on a bodge.

ALICIA. Señora, do you think you can help me?

YESENIA. Ali –

MARTA. Yes I can help you. Only if he were dead would I tell you, "Sorry very much pero no te puedo ayudar." Pero eso sí, esto te va a salir caro nena. It's going to cost you, esto es arroz con mango. Not so easy porque ya está enfrasca'o with this woman.

ALICIA. He's what with her?

YESENIA. He's obsessed. Like trapped. He's in there.

MARTA. Eso es.

ALICIA. I don't care how much it costs.

MARTA. Ah, no camina con los codos, la chacha. It didn't say in the guater that you were doing so good with money.

ALICIA. I'm not. But whatever it takes.

YESENIA. Ali…

ALICIA. I'll figure it out.

MARTA. I'm going to do something pero también tú va' a tener que hacer something too. We going to work together. ¿Ta'bien?

ALICIA. Yes. Whatever it takes. I'll do whatever you tell me to do.

MARTA. Cuidado chica. Don't tell people "guatever you want" or you could end up in a road that you don't want. Your love is big, eso se nota a leguas, but be careful you don't lose yourself in it.

ALICIA. I'm not going to lose myself, I'm trying to get myself back.

MARTA. Are you sure?

ALICIA. I'm trying to get myself and him back.

MARTA. Bueno, pa'que te digo que no si this is the main reason people come to me. Bring my lover back. Ah, que perdida de tiempo en mi opinion. Pero bueno. The first thing we gotta do is split them for good. Que se vaya la putita para un carajo. So I'm going to tell you sumsing to do. This you will do yourself. It's strong and it works good.

YESENIA. You cool with that? You said you didn't want to do anything like this to the girl.

ALICIA. Screw it, right? I mean, if we're going to do it, do it right.

YESENIA. You sure there.

MARTA. You want the recipe or no?

ALICIA. No, I do. I want it.

MARTA. Very good then. I'm going to give you este frasquito and you going to make a vinegar jar. Pero lo mas importante is that you have to go to his house and bury it under his doorstep.

YESENIA. ¿Cómo?

MARTA. Lo entierra' nena.

ALICIA. How? We have a cement doorstep. It's an apartment building.

MARTA. You find the closest tree or piece of dirt to the door. That's one. But he can't see you.

ALICIA. Well, of course. He'd think I'm nuts.

MARTA. Yes, that. And also, he can't see you. It won't work si te ve.

ALICIA. Okay…

MARTA. And the next thing is you got to get his esperma.

ALICIA. Pardon me?

MARTA. I need you to bring me his…you know, la lechita. His sperma.

ALICIA. How am I going to do that?

MARTA. Oh, you a smart girl. You just, you know…

> *(Does a jacking off motion.)*

Le chupas un poquito, you know men love that.

> *(The girls react. They're a little embarrassed.)*

Oh, but no sex. You can't put it in you or you'll be tied too. It has to be just from him. Not mixed together with your juice.

ALICIA. Ma'am, he won't see me. How can I get his sperm?

MARTA. Oh, you a pretty woman who is a smart girl. You will find a way. A little Jack Daniel's, un poco de mood lighting…you'll figure it out. I need this sperm to tie him to you. Para amarrarlo. Es lo mas fuerte. If you can't get his esperm, the next best thing es un calzonci'o sucio de el. Bring me any pair of dirty underwear, the dirtier the better and I can work with that too. Ponlo en ziploc, okey. Don't be walkin' around with that around the street.

ALICIA. …

YESENIA. Y Madrina, about how much will it be for this? How much are you going to charge for the – *(An abrupt doorbell.)*

MARTA. Sssshhh, chacha –

(She freezes. The doorbell again.)

Uy, chica. ¿Quién será? Nobody rings my bell, people I know come up the side like you. Unless it's the manayer. Uy give me that chacha. Put them in here.

(She frantically hides the cowrie shells and looks out the window.)

Esta desgraciada from across the hall probably told the manayer que yo hago esto and that I'm up to something in here. Three apartments they run me out of cuz I do this. It's not safe in Humboldt Park anymore.

(She looks out the window.)

¡Me cago en el cono de su madre! Chacha, hit the light. Apaga tú la luz. ¿Qué esperas?!

*(**YESENIA** turns off the lights.)*

Scene 5.2

REFLECTIONS OF A LULU #4

(Two areas. In one, **LULU** *is on her ball, bouncing. Facing upstage. In the second area,* **ALICIA** *is putting apple vinegar inside a jar. She writes something in a little piece of paper, spits in it, folds it thrice toward herself, and puts it in the jar.* **ALICIA** *closes the jar and shakes it.)*

The answer lies in nature! In the soil. In the air. The Earth gives you the tools!

(She turns around on her ball.)

That's the thing that makes the most sense, isn't it? That nature has put it all out there for you, like a puzzle. You just have to, you know...*do* the puzzle. Can't sleep? Drink some valerian root tea. Nature!

(Beat.)

Tummy hurts? Eat some ginger root. Eat of the same peppermint the Egyptians ate. It's been there for you since the beginning of time.

(Beat.)

Honey. This excretion of the noble honey bee to sweeten your tea, yes, but its larger purpose so grand and so intricate that it almost becomes Divine. Holy honey. To "sweeten" all kinds of *things*. Esoteric.

(Sucks on her sucker. Bounces with her back to us again.)

(Lights down.)

Scene 6

OPERATION STINKY DRAWERS

(Several days later. The girls are in **YESENIA***'s car.* **YESENIA***'s driving,* **ALICIA***'s in the passenger seat,* **LULU***'s eating in the back, and* **CAROLINA** *can be seen between the two front seats. They are staking out Diego's place.* **CAROLINA** *fiddles with the radio. She settles on something. They listen for a bit.)*

CAROLINA. If you had to name the best song of all time. I mean, if you had to pick the one song you thought was the absolute best humanity has come up with, what would you pick?

YESENIA. That's not even possible.

ALICIA. What's the criteria?

CAROLINA. Just the best song ever.

ALICIA. But are we talking Beethoven here or Donna Summer or Los Bukis or what? You have to give us a genre.

CAROLINA. Ultimate song of songs.

LULU. You'd have to take a statistical survey by population so perhaps, the most popular song in India would be, statistically speaking, the best song of all time.

CAROLINA. No, not like the most popular. Just the best.

LULU. Oh, then "Purple Haze." Jimi Hendrix.

YESENIA. No way! Shut up "Purple Haze." / Not even close.

ALICIA. "Purple Haze" is pretty much iconic there, Yessie.

YESENIA. That's not the best freakin' song of all time though. Something from the Beatles has to be like statistically the best song of all time. Even for India. Or like that song they play on New Year's.

LULU. "Auld Lang Syne."

YESENIA. *(To* **LULU***.)* Hey, what are you eating back there?

LULU. Sesame sticks. I made a whole batch. Want some?

(**LULU** *starts humming "Auld Lang Syne."*)

CAROLINA. Okay, then your personal favorite song. Let's not get lost in criteria. Just your favorite song.

YESENIA. *(Still to* **LULU.***)* What are sesame sticks? Stalking exes for more than an hour makes me hungry…

ALICIA. We're not stalking him. / I'm not even going in the house myself!

CAROLINA. Ay, why do you have to say it like that!

YESENIA. I'm just saying…

CAROLINA. Always just saying…

YESENIA. Get it straight. I don't mind stalking this fool out in the middle of a Thursday night. You know Thursday's Brazilian Hip Hop night at Sonoteque. But I'm here. I devised the plan myself. I'm here. I'm just saying I'm hungry. Shit. Can't I be hungry?

ALICIA. I should have packed us snacks.

YESENIA. I'm just saying…

LULU. Would you like some of my delicious sesame sticks?

(**YESENIA** *takes some reluctantly. Hey, they're not bad.*)

CAROLINA. Are we sure the party's tonight?

ALICIA. Yeah. It's tonight.

YESENIA. These are so good. Are these fried?

LULU. Baked.

ALICIA. You know, I had already gotten a dress for that party. I just needed to get some red shoes. It's so funny, on Tuesday he even mentions it to me. Here I get so excited because he finally asked me out to talk. Like, I didn't have to beg him or…well, not beg, but I didn't have to try to get him to see me, you know. It came from him. And the whole meal was going so well, we were being so careful and civil and then he mentions the party and I kind of get a little –

YESENIA. Cabrón.

CAROLINA. Te ilusionaste, sure.

ALICIA. Yeah. It all just went down the drain after that. All that progress.

>   *(Pause.)*

CAROLINA. Ooh, girl, you need to do your roots.

ALICIA. Who thinks about roots anymore.

>   *(Pause.)*

>   (CAROLINA *begins to sing "Luka" by Suzanne Vega.* **LULU** joins her halfway.)*

CAROLINA. That's my favorite song.

LULU. Yeah, that's a good one…

ALICIA. I liked her and Depeche Mode. That was my deep phase.

YESENIA. My deep and angry phase was Wu Tang… Shit, I might have to pee.

CAROLINA. You always have to pee or poo or something. Are you sure you're not a diabetic?

YESENIA. I have a small bladder. No me eches la sal, that my grandma's a diabetic.

CAROLINA. You should carry a bed pan in your purse.

YESENIA. I'm gonna smack you on your nose.

>   *(Pause.)*

CAROLINA. Guys… Can we go over the plan again?

YESENIA. Cono…carajo…

ALICIA. It's not hard. Yesenia has my key so she goes in and grabs a pair of his underwear from the hamper while Lulu and I hurry to bury the jar by that tree. You stay in

---

*A license to produce *Enfrascada* does not include a performance license for "Luka." The publisher and author suggest that the licensee contact ASCAP or BMI to ascertain the music publisher and contact such music publisher to license or acquire permission for performance of the song. If a license or permission is unattainable for "Luka" the licensee may not use the song in *Enfrascada* but may create an original composition in a similar style. For further information, please see Music Use Note on page 3.

the car looking out and you call us if you see anything fishy. Everyone will have their cell phones out. Except for Lulu, who doesn't have one.

YESENIA. Who the hell doesn't have a cell phone in 2011?

CAROLINA. Why does Yesenia get to steal the underwear and I stay in the car?!

YESENIA. Because I got nerves of steel and won't get all scared.

ALICIA. That and you know Bandido loves her and won't make a fuss.

LULU. Bandido's such a nice name. It has just the right amount of syllables. Ban-dee-dough.

ALICIA. So we're all clear. Caro?

LULU. The shovel?

ALICIA. I got it. Well, it's this.

(*Takes out little shovel.*)

I got gloves, I got a bottle of water to make the dirt soft. I thought of everything. I'm like fucking MacGyver right now.

CAROLINA. What happens if when I'm in the car a cop passes by? And I'm just hanging out in a car looking suspicious? This isn't my car. What do I do if they flash their lights on me and start harassing me like on *Cops*?

YESENIA. You talk on your cell phone. And look real animated like you're in the middle of a conversation and that's why you're parked. OKAY?

CAROLINA. (*Slowly.*) Like acting. Oooh, that's good. Okay, I accept being the "lookout."

(*Beat.*)

Oh, you know what would be good? I wish I had one of those pirate lookout binoculars for just the one eye? I'd like to have one of those.

YESENIA. You watch too much TV, Caro. You need a part-time job, need to do something with your life. You have too much time on your hands. This one, sitting there all day watching TV in her fluffy couch. I don't know what the hell you do all day.

ALICIA. Caro, I'd love to have your life.

(**CAROLINA**'s *hurt.*)

CAROLINA. Yeah, my life is a fairy tale.

ALICIA. Don't have to work. You have a great guy who's crazy about you. And you got him wrapped around your finger. Anything you want, it's yours. I'd say it was pretty fairy tale.

(*This affects* **CAROLINA**. *She abruptly changes the radio station and bumps* **YESENIA**.)

YESENIA. Watch it. Just ask.

(*They listen to the radio for a bit.*)

LULU. "*After silence, that which comes nearest to expressing the inexpressible is music.*"

(**YESENIA** *abruptly turns the radio off. Everyone's getting kind of testy. Pause.*)

(**LULU** *begins to sing "Luka" by Suzanne Vega.***)

CAROLINA. You know something? Ever since you and Diego broke up…

(*Beat.*)

You really think it's just easy breezy for me? Ali, everything costs me. My life costs me. You know what, let me stop.

(*Pause.*)

**A license to produce *Enfrascada* does not include a performance license for "Luka." The publisher and author suggest that the licensee contact ASCAP or BMI to ascertain the music publisher and contact such music publisher to license or acquire permission for performance of the song. If a license or permission is unattainable for "Luka" the licensee may not use the song in *Enfrascada* but may create an original composition in a similar style. For further information, please see Music Use Note on page 3.

You haven't asked me IN WEEKS about Vic and me. /
Not once.

YESENIA. What are you talking about? The only maldita
cosa we talk about is Vic and you!

CAROLINA. Not you!

YESENIA. Are you about to get your period?

>	*(CAROLINA smacks YESENIA from the back.)*

YESENIA. Aaauu…

>	*(Pause.)*

LULU. *"Action is the antidote to despair."*

YESENIA. What the hell is that? Seriously, do you sit there
memorizing shit just so you can confuse everybody!
This is why I never liked academics. I dated a dude,
head of some department at UIC? Never got him. Never
knew what the fuck he was talking about. We would get
into it and he'd always say "We are not arguing, we are
having a polemic." Got on my nerves!

LULU. *(To ALICIA.)* She wants you to ask her what's wrong.

ALICIA. Thank you for the translation, Lulu.

LULU. Oh. You're welcome.

CAROLINA. I don't need you to ask me, but it would just be
nice if…

YESENIA. I still don't understand what this big revolu is all
about.

CAROLINA. You know what, Yesenia? You're being a
cabrona right now. You know exactly what's going on,
and what's more, you know exactly why I haven't been
able to share it, yet here you are being a total bitch to
me. Osea…

>	*(Beat.)*

YESENIA. Sorry. Being all closed up is gettin' me all
claustrophobic.

LULU. What haven't you been able to share?

CAROLINA. …

ALICIA. …

YESENIA. I been thinking something.

ALICIA. Well, call the Trib.

YESENIA. Whoa. Now what did I do to you?

ALICIA. Nothing. Fuck, why can't they just come out already!

YESENIA. Listen, and Ali, don't be like "Forget you, Yesenia," cuz I'm here for the long haul but haven't you noticed that lately, all we talk about is dudes? Well, not you Lulu. I never know what the hell you're talking about. But both of you. Aren't you guys getting a little bored? Now don't make a face, Ali. I'm going to go in there and grab those drawers and help you bury this motherfucking jar but seriously I was thinking that. Aren't you fucking tired of it? When did we become those girls? When did we become our mothers waiting at the kitchen table? We got nothing better to do than talk about dudes?! Real talk. I will never let a man rule my nights and days. My papi's dead and that's the last guy who had any right to tell me what to do. My papi was the last good man on Earth.

  (To the sky.)

Bendición, Papi.

  (Pause.)

ALICIA. Maybe we should go.

YESENIA. No, ya pa'que. We're here now. I was just saying. In general. Don't you feel a little derailed?

LULU. Holla, ho, Curtis! The villain's near.

  (She means Diego and Bethany are coming out of the apartment.)

YESENIA. Oh, shit. There they are. Get down you two. Duck Ali. Con disímulo. Oh, look at that hijo de puta. And to think he was my football buddy. What the fuck is she wearing?

CAROLINA. Yuck, look at those shoes. Payless much?

LULU. That's a lot of leg for one dress.

CAROLINA. Trash.

ALICIA. She's not ugly at all.

CAROLINA. Are you kidding me?

ALICIA. No, you guys told me she was ugly!

CAROLINA. Look at the pig nose. You can see those nostrils from here.

YESENIA. You think they can see us?

LULU. The night is our cloak.

ALICIA. He doesn't look unhappy. Why is he not unhappy? He should be miserable, like I'm miserable.

(*Car lights. Tire sounds. They watch.*)

LULU. The coast is clear.

CAROLINA. Ali, are you okay?

ALICIA. I want to fuck him up. I want to fuck her up. I want to fuck with their lives so hard they won't know what hit them.

CAROLINA. Ali...

YESENIA. Now we're talking. Now we're talking. Alright, but first we handle our shit. Come on. Everybody got what they're supposed to do, right? Lulu, you make the hole and Ali prays over it like Doña Marta told her; I go in and grab a pair of calzoncillos from the hamper; wipe the doorknobs; Caro, grab your phone and let us know of anything that looks fishy.

CAROLINA. What if they realize they've forgotten something and they come back like in the movies?

YESENIA. I'm going to smack you on your nose! Just call us if anything's suspect.

(*Beat.*)

Ali? You with us, Alicia?

ALICIA. Abso-fucking-lutely.

YESENIA. Okay, Operation Stinky Drawers begins, a la una, a las dos y a las-GO!

(Lights down.)

Scene 7

CIHUANAHUALLI: QUEEN OF JARS

(A couple of weeks later. ALICIA is standing in the threshold of KARINA's kichen, who is in the middle of some kind of prayer/chant thing. KARINA is mid limpia and there is a MUCHACHA standing in the middle of the room with her eyes shut and her palms pointing upward. KARINA is holding a bouquet of perejil and gestures for ALICIA to enter and close the door. KARINA points to a corner where she should stand and never stops praying under her breath. ALICIA tries to stand there and not take up too much space. KARINA resumes the limpia [spiritual cleaning].)

(KARINA chants in Nahuatl.)

(KARINA starts to clean ALICIA and whack her with the bouquet. The MUCHACHA starts crying. We can't understand their chanting but it gets intense.)

…muy fuerte lo que traes…

(The MUCHACHA starts gagging and keeling over in pain.)

Pero de qué te lo sacamos te lo sacamos.

(KARINA holds the MUCHACHA's stomach and prays on it. The MUCHACHA cries. KARINA begins to utter some final prayers over the belly. At that moment CAROLINA knocks on the door and lets herself in. She notices the ritual and quietly goes to kiss ALICIA on the cheek. They observe. KARINA finishes. The poor MUCHACHA is kind of a mess.)

Muchacha, lo que tú traes, lo traes de niña. Mucho muy fuerte. Mierda que le pusieron a tu madre. Bueno pero ya, no llores. Ya te saqué casi todo. No llores.

(The MUCHACHA takes out a little package, something wrapped in a handkerchief. KARINA takes it, kisses it to her forehead, and puts it in her cleavage.)

MUCHACHA. Gracias, Karina. De veras, muchísimas gracias.

(KARINA wraps the bouquet in some newspaper and gives it to the MUCHACHA.)

KARINA. Sí para eso estamos, muchacha. Ándale pues, y te acuerdas como te dije. Lo tiras en el rio o el lago.

(The poor hot mess of a MUCHACHA takes the bundle and nods. She hugs KARINA and kind of awkwardly acknowledges the girls as she goes out the door.)

Pobrecita. Trae una maldición de familia. Eso ya viene de la madre o la abuela. No sé. Pásenle, siéntense. ¿En qué les puedo ayudar? ¿Ella es tu amiga? Hola mucho gusto.

ALICIA. Hi. Hola. ¿Cómo estás?

KARINA. Verygoodandyouthankyouverymuch. Es todo lo que puedo decir en inglés.

(A crash is heard offstage, then a couple of kids crying.)

Ay, estos chamacos. ¿Me aguantan un tantito? Ahorititia regreso.

CAROLINA. Pásale Karina. Pásale.

(KARINA exits.)

Those are her kids, they are a handful. Oh, I forgot to warn you. They're *special* too, so don't…like don't think badly about them while they're around. They got like little powers too. So just watch what you think around them, okay? Oh, my God, one time the little one got so mad at me – I didn't let him play with my BlackBerry or something. He was like the Hulk. Looked like he was about to turn green.

(Does an impression.)

CAROLINA. Well, I don't think anything of it and then we're in the middle of my reading and I get this pang on my side. And I'm like, "Ouch." Karina notices and she asks me really calm, "When did you start hurting. Was it before or after Lalito wanted to play with your phone?" "After," I said. Then she goes, "Lalito, cuatla cuatla cuatla." Oh, that's my version of Nahuatl, I'm not being disrespectful.

ALICIA. That's what?

CAROLINA. It's like Aztec. She speaks like indigenous to them. Any way the little kid comes and puts his hand on my side very Damien-like and the pain goes away. Swear to God.

ALICIA. Shut up. You're scaring me.

CAROLINA. Shut up. I'm scaring myself. Shut up. Why did I tell that story?

(Shudders.)

No she's great. She's got like a real gift. I'm not even kidding you. Hey I tried to call you on your phone but I kept getting a weird message?

ALICIA. Yeah, I know. I have to pay that.

*(We can hear **KARINA** speaking to her kids in Nahuatl.)*

KARINA. *(Offstage.)* Nahuatzi otzi huizcolini. Natzi? *[Que no te cache haciendo maldades otra vez porque le voy a decir a tu papá. ¿Me entiendes?]*

CAROLINA. I told you, "Cuatli cuatlacohitl." It sounds so cool.

KARINA. *(Entering kitchen.)* Disculpen. Qué pena. Qué pena con ustedes.

CAROLINA. No te preocupes Karina.

*(To **ALICIA**.)*

You want me to translate everything or just what you don't understand.

ALICIA. I don't know. Everything I guess. Just, translate everything.

(**KARINA** *starts gathering the cards but stops. Looks intently at* **ALICIA**.)

KARINA. Uy, tu amiga trae algo pesado...

(She burps.)

CAROLINA. She says you have something heavy. You bring something heavy. Oh, FYI, when she starts to burp, that's not a good sign. FYI.

ALICIA. Why? What does it mean?

CAROLINA. She's like getting your bad stuff out. And she can taste it or something.

ALICIA. What?

CAROLINA. Yeah, it's deep.

(**KARINA** *is touching* **ALICIA**'s *head. La soba. Sometimes* **ALICIA** *looks at* **CAROLINA** *in confusion, and* **CAROLINA** *just nods.*)

KARINA. *(Burping.)* Aaay...hhhmmm.

(To **CAROLINA**.)

Ella está mucho muy bloqueada.

CAROLINA. She says you're very blocked.

KARINA. Me deja que la sobe con un huevo?

CAROLINA. Can she rub you down with an egg? No, it's okay. It's like a spiritual cleaning. You need it girl.

(To **KARINA**.)

Si está bién, Karina.

ALICIA. Am I going to stink? I don't want to get egg stains on this shirt.

CAROLINA. No, she doesn't like break the egg. You'll see.

KARINA. ¿Sabes, qué? Primero consultemos las cartas. Vi algunas cositas que no me gustaron.

CAROLINA. She says she's going to ask the cards first about some little things she didn't like.

ALICIA. That she didn't like about me?

CAROLINA. That she saw just now while she was touching you.

ALICIA. Like how does she mean?

CAROLINA. ¿Cómo qué?

KARINA. Ahorita vemos. Barajealas.

CAROLINA. Shuffle.

KARINA. En tres partes.

CAROLINA. Split into three parts.

KARINA. Pon la mano arriba.

CAROLINA. Put your hand...no, your *right* hand – on top of the deck. Always your right hand.

KARINA. Repíte. Díme la verdad la verdad y nada más que la verdad.

CAROLINA. Say, "Tell me the truth, the truth and nothing but the truth."

ALICIA. Who am I saying it to?

CAROLINA. Out to the cosmos. To the universe. Just say it, "Tell me the truth, the truth and nothing but the truth."

ALICIA. Tell me the truth, the truth and nothing but the truth.

  (Beat.)

I feel like saying, "So help me God."

CAROLINA. No, don't say that. You're not in court.

  *(**KARINA** begins the card reading. She reacts to the first cards.)*

KARINA. Ya. Sí. Sí. Ella trae mucha revoltura.

CAROLINA. She's saying that you're all jumbled.

ALICIA. Okay.

KARINA. No debería traer tanta revoltura. Ella es una persona quien tenía los pies firmemente plantados en la tierra, pero ahorita...

(Reading some more.)

KARINA. Ya. Ya. Ella tiene una desilusión amorosa y se está perdiendo en su propia tiniebla.

CAROLINA. Oh, shoot. What the hell's tiniebla? Okay, hold on. She said that you shouldn't be so jumbled because usually you're a person who has her feet firmly planted on the ground but that you had a love disillusionment, heartbreak. You have heartbreak and that you are losing yourself in your own tiniebla.

(Beat.)

Fog! You're lost in a fog. How could I forget fog?

(She sets down more cards. A crashing noise is heard from offstage. A kid cries.)

KARINA. Ay, disculpen. Lalito!

(Heading to the room where the kids are.)

Yumanajatzi. Donatiu. Donatiu! [Ya les dije que se pongan sosiegos. Les voy a pegar. ¡Les voy a pegar!]

(Beat.)

Bueno, ¿en dónde quedamos? A ver.

(Throws more cards.)

Ah, Ya.

(More cards.)

Ya. Es buena muchacha, verdad. Sí, pero ella va a perderlo todo si no deja de seguir a ese hombre. Ella no debería estarlo siguiendo así.

(Pause.)

ALICIA. ¿Caro? Something about losing?

CAROLINA. Yeah. You have to stop chasing Diego, she says. Ali, I promise I haven't talked to her about this.

KARINA. Veo aquí que ella acaba de tener una cama con él.

CAROLINA. Alicia, did you just sleep with him?!

ALICIA. *(This captures her attention more than anything.)* What?

CAROLINA. She's saying that it says that you just slept with him not too long ago. Did you sleep with Diego?

ALICIA. Yeah.

CAROLINA. When? / He's still over there with the other…

ALICIA. What else does she say?

CAROLINA. Oh, my God.

ALICIA. All this is working Caro, I can't let up. If it's the last thing I do, he's going to come back to me. I just need something stronger.

(*About* **KARINA**.)

She's very good. I didn't tell anyone that.

KARINA. Aquí me dice que este hombre no va a dejar a la nueva. Ellos estan enlazados ya. Ella se va a embarazar.

CAROLINA. Great. She says that he's not leaving the new one. And that she's going to get pregnant.

ALICIA. What? No. No no. She can't get pregnant. We were going to get pregnant. Before all this, we were going to… No. Tell her she has to do something to help me. Something strong. I don't care how dark. I don't care. And that she has to fuck that little bitch up. Fuck that pregnancy up. She has to help me. Tell her.

(*Beat.*)

Usted me ayuda por favor. Por favor me ayuda.

CAROLINA. Dice que…

KARINA. No, no tienes que interpretar, ya le entendí. Tú quieres que te lo amarre, bien amarradito.

(**CAROLINA** *doesn't translate right away.*)

ALICIA. Caro…

CAROLINA. She's asking if you want her to…if you want her to bind him to you, real good.

ALICIA. Sí. That's exactly what I want. I want you to bind him to me. No matter what.

CAROLINA. Don't say that, Alicia.

ALICIA. What do I have to do? / ¿Qué hacer?

CAROLINA. I'm telling you from experience Alicia, you don't want to do that.

KARINA. Bueno.

(She throws more cards.)

Mira, yo puedo hacer lo que ella quiera ¿pero te puedo dar un mal consejo? Tiene que dejar de estar jalando a este hombre. Porque esto, por algo paso.

CAROLINA. She says she can do whatever you want but that she wants to advise you that you have to stop pulling this man to you. That this happened for a reason. Ali, she's saying this happened for a good reason.

KARINA. Aquí se ve que ella lo esta jalando espiritualmente con muchos trabajos. Pero van a terminar atraparapándola si no se pone trucha.

CAROLINA. That with all the spells you're doing on him, you're the one who's going to end up trapped if you're not careful.

ALICIA. Can she do something really strong that works? The strongest she can do.

*(**CAROLINA** doesn't say anything. To **KARINA**.)*

Por favor. Ayuda.

KARINA. Bueno, yo nadamás quería decirte eso. Te amarramos a este macho entonces.

CAROLINA. She said she just wanted to warn you. But that she'll do it.

*(Noise from the kids' room. **KARINA** stands up and declares something in Nahuatl that shuts the kids down immediately.)*

KARINA. *(Standing up, hands to the sky.)* Yumanajatzi. Tutetzinei. Yumanajatzi. [Calm down! I will bust your mouth open!]*

(Silence.)

Disculpen. Bueno. Me vas a tener que conseguir un frasco grande.

CAROLINA. You're going to have to find a big jar.

ALICIA. Jars are no problem. I have a million jars. I'm the queen of jars.

CAROLINA. *(To* KARINA.*)* Qué okay.

    (Lights down.)

Scene 7.2

REFLECTIONS OF A LULU #5

*(Two areas. In one, **LULU** is on the floor by her ball, with her books on the floor. She's in the middle of jotting something. In the second area, **ALICIA** is surrounded by jars. She's in a sea of jars, okay a table/altar thing full of jars. She's shaking the first jar. Shaking that honey jar like a pro, chanting something. Looking a little possessed.)*

It stands to reason, the concept of energies. Vibrations…um, vibes. Strong essences. Scientists call it the collective intelligence of cells, some call it by other names. Whatever it is, it has a design rooted in what we cannot understand. But we mess with that design. I think we walk around in each other's cipher way too much. Maybe we weren't meant for crowded spaces. Or we attempt to manipulate these essences for gain or convenience.

(Beat.)

Diabetes. Here because we had to refine sugar! Why did we need to go and do a thing like that for? Cancer. Ancient man never experienced cancer. (Or rarely did.) Cancer is of our own modern design! Oooh…

(She jots something down in her notebook.)

And the spirit. The spirit is as real as the body, so what is a cancer of the spirit? Of the soul? And is there a cure?

*(She stares toward **ALICIA** then jots the following down.)*

Note, look up…"being cursed."

(Lights down.)

Scene 8

R.I.P.

(It's dusk at the cemetery. Yeah, a cemetery.
CAROLINA *is texting on her BlackBerry. She's*
getting spooked by all the noises of the night. **LULU**
is with her, kneeling by a grave.)

CAROLINA. Of course. Now nobody is answering. Imagine
if I would have come alone? Thank God for you, Lulu.
Imagine?

LULU. Oh, I love cemeteries.

CAROLINA. But did Ali have to drag us down here right
when it's about to get dark? We were going to sneak in
anyway. I don't understand why we couldn't have come
early in the morning. Come here, Lulu. You're too far
away. No te me pierdas.

> *(LULU obeys.)*

You don't mind if I grab you by your arm like this, do
you?

LULU. Cozy.

CAROLINA. These gravestones are stressing me out, Lulu!
Are you too young to remember "Thriller"? Sometimes
I forget that some people only know the crazy baby
dangling Michael Jackson.

LULU. Who doesn't know "Thriller."

> *(Some time during* **CAROLINA**'s *talking,* **YESENIA**
> *and* **ALICIA** *have come in, so they catch the last bit*
> *of the "Thriller" conversation.* **YESENIA** *playfully*
> *decides to scare* **CAROLINA** *in her best Vincent*
> *Price voice.* **CAROLINA** *flips the fuck out.)*

CAROLINA. Aaaahhh!

> *(She begins to pound* **YESENIA** *with her hands and*
> *purse after she realizes it's her.)*

(Next three lines overlap.)

YESENIA. WHAT THE HELL!

ALICIA. Jesus, Carolina. Come on!

CAROLINA. I hate you so much! YOU SCARED ME.

YESENIA. You scared ME, shit! Well so much for not getting caught.

CAROLINA. You jerk! I swear my life just flashed before my eyes right there.

YESENIA. I think you just woke up Deborah Silverstein there, 1934 to 1999, con tus gritos.

CAROLINA. *(Shuddering. Shaking her hands and feet)* Shutupshutupshutup.

(Kiss salutations all around. Of course.)

ALICIA. You a little spooked Caro? Hey, cus'. Did you guys pay the spirit?

YESENIA. I put a dime by the entrance. Not a silver dime. But I put a dime.

CAROLINA. I put a silver dollar. Just in case. You know. Don't worry, Lulu. I paid for both of us.

YESENIA. You gave the ghost a tip?

CAROLINA. Always err on the side of over tipping is what my father taught me. So I left a silver dollar.

YESENIA. It's supposed to be a dime. I think the number ten is the thing.

CAROLINA. I think the silver's the thing. I was there when Karina told us to put una moneda de plata.

ALICIA. I had to go to a coin shop on Archer and then to one in Chinatown. I got an actual silver dime. Cost me a fortune.

YESENIA. You are so literal. It's just the gesture that counts.

ALICIA. I want to do this right.

CAROLINA. I think the whole thing's up for interpretation, you know? Because the spirit guarding the gate has to take inflation into consideration.

YESENIA. You keep yapping, you're going to wake up the dead. And it's going to be like "Thriller" up in here.

(She does a quick "Thriller" move, with the eyes.)

Buuuaaahaaahaaahhaa.

CAROLINA. Ali, tell her to stop that!

ALICIA. Yessie.

YESENIA. What am I doing?

ALICIA. Don't scare her.

YESENIA. "Thriller" scares her? What a wuss.

LULU. If you want, we could bang on something, Carolina. The Saxons used to bang on things to scare away the dead.

YESENIA. Sure, let's just invite the po-po to our little tombstone pizza party.

ALICIA. Yessie, did you bring rum?

YESENIA. Cheap ass Captain Morgan, but it's rum.

ALICIA. That's good enough.

CAROLINA. I have the angel food cake you said to get.

ALICIA. Good, thanks. I have the black bag.

(Taking out the honey jar she's been shaking for months.)

And now to find a gravestone for the jar.

(ALICIA starts looking.)

LULU. You know, technically this is not a graveyard. It's a cemetery. A graveyard is always on the same grounds as a church. This is on the same grounds as a Burger King.

CAROLINA. So wait, is one like less holy than the other?

ALICIA. Ladies, I think I need to do my thing now so… Shh.

YESENIA. Alright then. Let's not make it a big production. Let's pick a grave and go.

ALICIA. No, Yesenia. Stop. It has to be me, okay? Seriously, please don't screw around. / I have to go grave by grave. Find one that feels right and ask permission to bury this there. Make my petition.

YESENIA.   **CAROLINA.**
 Oh, excuse me.   Yessie, just let her.

CAROLINA. Wait, you're going to bury it?

ALICIA. Well, I'm going to leave it by the grave with the offerings.

> *(We hear a noise of some sort.* **CAROLINA** *shrieks, the other two freeze.)*

CAROLINA. Ay, Dios Santo!

YESENIA. ¡Coño! No seas miedosa. / It was a bird flying.

ALICIA. Oh, my God, you just gave me a heart attack.

CAROLINA. Sorry. Sorry. Ali, start talking to them, so we can get the heck out of here.

ALICIA. Yeah, why don't I do that.

> *(She starts walking around carefully looking at graves. She kneels by one and holds her jar. A while before anyone talks.)*

LULU. Did you know in ancient times all corpses / were buried facing east?

CAROLINA. Oooh, don't say corpses.

LULU. They did. It was believed that from the east would come the Final Judgment.

CAROLINA. ...

LULU. Also, it was believed that spirits, or ghosts could only travel in a straight line so funeral processions never took the same route back to their houses so the spirits wouldn't follow them.

CAROLINA. Shoot, I'm taking Lake Shore Drive back to the house.

YESENIA. Fuck. I gotta pee.

CAROLINA. Don't pee on a grave. You'll piss off a ghost y te saca la mano while you're peeing and grab you in your cosita.

YESENIA. *(Laughing.)* Shut up.

ALICIA. Sssshh…

> *(Long pause while they look around.)*

YESENIA. *(Reading a grave.)* "In loving memory." You know, we're all going to end up here one day.

CAROLINA. Don't say that.

YESENIA. It's true.

CAROLINA. I know, but don't say that.

YESENIA. In loving memory. What's mine going to say? Yesenia Rivera, good friend, great real estate agent, wife to none.

CAROLINA. It's going to say more than that. Don't depress yourself.

LULU. It's going to say Yesenia Rivera, ebullient, vivacious spirit. The world will not be the same without her.

> *(YESENIA has a little moment with LULU. She blushes or something. While the girls have been talking ALICIA has found her grave.)*

ALICIA. I think this is the one.

> *(They all go join her.)*

YESENIA. *(Reading grave.)* Stacey Lynn Whitmore. 2001 to 2006.

> *(Beat.)*

Oh, shit.

ALICIA. It's the first one that speaks to me.

CAROLINA. Ali, that's a baby's grave. Don't…don't do it on a baby's grave, okay?

ALICIA. No, I feel really good about this grave.

CAROLINA. I don't feel right about you doing this on a baby's grave.

YESENIA. Yeah, maybe there's another grave we could, you know…there's a ton over here.

ALICIA. This is the one.

CAROLINA. Alicia, not from a baby's grave.

(CAROLINA holds her stomach protectively.)

ALICIA. No, it's this one. Give me the angel food cake. I think that's better than the rum in this case.

CAROLINA. I'm not going to give you cake to put on this baby's grave.

ALICIA. It wasn't a baby. She was five.

CAROLINA. Are you listening to yourself? Ali, I think we've officially gone too far here.

ALICIA. Carolina, can I just have the cake please?

CAROLINA. No, I think that this is getting out of hand. You're about to desecrate / the grave of a...

ALICIA. If you don't want to be here, you don't have to be here, okay?

CAROLINA. ...

ALICIA. I will leave the rum if you won't give me the cake.

YESENIA. No! I don't think you should leave rum for a baby, Ali.

ALICIA. What is wrong with you two?

LULU. Cousin, look where you are standing and look what you're about to do.

　　　(Beat.)

"Grace be with you."

CAROLINA. I think Karina was right, Ali. I think you're losing yourself a little bit. The Alicia I know would understand that she is crossing a line by putting that jar on that baby's grave. Shoot, the Alicia I know wouldn't ever be in a cemetery in the first place! I can't believe I'm about to say this, but I miss the Alicia who didn't believe in all this. / She reasoned.

ALICIA. Are you serious right now?

YESENIA. I do too, Ali.

ALICIA. You fucking hypocrites. Both of you. After all that shit. After all you pushed.

YESENIA. I know, man. I know. I just never thought we'd end up at a cemetery, you know?

ALICIA. I don't think you realize what this whole thing has done to me. What it took from me. / I don't think you realize...

CAROLINA. Yeah, it took you! You're gone, Ali. And so fast that it's kind of scary. Amiga, I'm sure it hurts like hell. Jeez, it's your whole life, you know? Your whole life came crashing down and you had to try to fix it. I get it. I do. And out of anyone here, I'm the most in support of your methods to get him back. Come on, you've seen me...

(She stomps.)

...do all sorts of craziness with Vic. I get that. What I don't get is this. What are you doing? This isn't you. The way you've been handling yourself with Diego. / It's not you. It's cheap. You're sleeping with him while he's still with that girl.

ALICIA. Shut up, Carolina!

YESENIA. Wait, what?!

CAROLINA. How can you disrespect yourself like that? / What is your life about right now, amiga? You're about nothing but jars, right now. You talk about nothing but jars. Te enfrascaste a ti misma amiga.

ALICIA. You know what, Carolina? You know what...

(Beat.)

CAROLINA. Ali, a guy shouldn't take over your whole life like that.

ALICIA. Look who's fucking talking! Mrs. Betty Homemaker who's done nothing with her life except trap a man. What are you stuck in 1951?

YESENIA. Whoa, Ali. Easy there.

(Pause. This broke CAROLINA*'s heart. Like in pieces.)*

CAROLINA. You're right. No...you're right. I'm a total joke. You know what? I think I should go. Lulu, you want to come or… I mean, I'll be in the car, you're welcome to come.

(She starts to go.)

CAROLINA. Alicia, he's not leaving her. He's about to have a baby with this girl and babies, they seal the deal. Trust me. They seal the deal. He doesn't want you and nothing you do is going to make him want you again.

(Heavy, heavy pause.)

LULU. *You seldom sit at a crossroads and know it's a / crossroads…*

ALICIA. Lulu! Can you please! Not right now, please. Sorry.

CAROLINA. Okay. Yeah. I'll be at…yeah.

(LULU exits. She kind of runs off.)

ALICIA. Oh, you too?

YESENIA. All I'm going to say is that you're about to have nothing left if you keep this shit up. I'm going to wait in the car –

ALICIA. You don't have to wait in the fucking car, I'll take a –

YESENIA. I'm going to wait in the motherfucking car for you! Because I'm your girl. And Caro's your girl. And I'm going to wait in the fucking car.

(YESENIA leaves the rum by ALICIA's feet. ALICIA is left all alone holding her honey jar. Suddenly it weighs so much. Suddenly it's made of poisonous stuff. She sees it as if for the first time. A long moment. What the fuck has just happened? And then, unexpectedly, she opens the honey jar! The lights shift, something happens. Are those voices we hear when she opens the jar? Is that Diego? Is it the wise words of the three magi? It's something. Something escapes from that jar and when it does, ALICIA suddenly starts to cry. Oh, man. Does she ever start to cry. She cries, and cries, and cries a

*little more. Then, right before the lights go down, it
is good. Good seeps in. It's a good cry.)*

Fin